HUNTED BY THE LION

AN M/M FAIRYTALE ROMANCE

AMELIA HAYDEN

HUNTED

BY THE
LION

An M/M Fairytale Romance

(Once Upon a Time)

Cover Art by DoElle Designs
Subtitle & Chapter Break Images by Opal Reyne

CHAPTER ONE
DIANA

The high-pitched giggle floating in through my window was making me reach my limit on my sister's antics. A glance out the window showed me the perfect view of a couple's outing. The two of them sat on the grass, happily engaged in conversation. I scoffed and shook my head.

How she managed to get so many suitors was beyond me, yet every month there was a new man at our door asking for a chance to see the "Beauty of Illia city". Illia, a town known for how small and quaint it was. And CiCi loved the attention enough to play to each man's ego, letting them chase after her.

This latest one seemed to be lasting longer than the others. Most bored her, after a few weeks, but this guy had been going strong for almost three months now. Part of me hoped that CiCi would finally get married, so I could stop hearing about the men courting her. Another part of me knew it would just open up a whole other mess of problems.

If CiCi were to marry, that would officially make me a spinster. At least according to society. My father would go along with it. I would be shunned and sent to Aunt Camillia's house up north. Not that I wouldn't mind it. Aunt Camillia accepts me for who I am. I could dress how I wanted and do the things I enjoyed. She never had a bad word to say about me being me.

I wouldn't be stuck having to wear these uncomfortable dresses and spend my days sewing. I could wear pants and break out of these corsets. And Aunt Camillia would appreciate that I could hunt better than most of the men around here. It wouldn't be something I had to hide, pretending all the time that my father was the great huntsman of the area.

Still absently staring out the window where the giggles have now turned into squeals, I let my mind wander to what I could be; what I could do. I see my sister jumping up and down as a ring is placed on her finger.

I saw it happening, but my mind doesn't register it. My thoughts go back to what I could do if my sister were married off. Maybe I could go by a name that felt right. Maybe a masculine name, instead of...

"Diana!" My sister's squeals precede her into the house. When she turns the corner, her face is so bright. "Look!"

She holds up her hand, making a pit lodge in my stomach. A sparkling diamond ring in the shape of a rose graces her left ring finger. I know I saw it happening, but my mind was in a whole different world. A world where I hoped I could be me. Maybe now I can be me, who I really am meant to be.

"I'm getting married!" CiCi circles the room in excited energy. Her hands wave wildly as her words continue, "Isn't this wonderful?"

She looks at me expectantly. My words are stiff as they leave my lips, "Yes, of course."

It seems I would be going to live with Aunt Camillia. Part of me is relieved to finally have the decision made, even if it means a life of loneliness. I can deal with being lonely, if I can be myself through it.

Another squeal escapes her as she runs over to grab my hands, her voice dropping to a whisper, "And guess what?"

I raise my brows in question. I wouldn't even venture a guess. My sister is always full of surprises.

"He's a prince!"

My heart chills. "No," my words are barely a breath. "Are you sure?"

She nods her head and holds up the ring. "See it's the insignia for the Roselani kingdom. Kellen said it's been the betrothal ring passed down through his family for generations. Can you believe it?"

A prince? How could she not have told me? If CiCi marries a prince, there is no way father will let me disappear off to Auntie's. Not when our family will be under the scrutiny of an entire kingdom.

I jolt as CiCi grabs my hands; I am no longer paying attention to her words. "I can't wait for you to find your own prince, Diana. Then we can be beautiful brides together."

No. No, that's the last thing I want. Not that I don't want to get married, but I don't want to be a bride. Yet, in all my years I never could get the courage to tell that to CiCi. I couldn't tell anyone. This is news that is frowned upon in our society.

"Where-where is this prince?"

I need to know how much of a prince he is. Like is he a prince in a small kingdom. Or a *PRINCE* that is going to have our family in the spotlight for the rest of our lives. I am hoping for the former. I want to be out of the spotlight, eventually.

"He had to leave. Some man came here on a massive horse and called him away. I think he said that Kellen's father was sick. He promised to come back once he was better, so he could introduce me to his father."

I watch as CiCi runs off to tell our father.

I sit and think to myself. I can't marry a prince as a woman. I don't feel like a woman. I feel like a man, but my body is that of a beautiful woman. This isn't who I want to be. I would love to find a prince, or any man, for that matter, who will accept me as the person I feel like I am on the inside.

The man of my dreams would accept me as I am. He wouldn't want me dolled up in fancy gowns or tending to his babies. He would want me as the man I really feel like, on the inside. Maybe I could even become the man I am supposed to be, then I would know he'd truly accepts me for who I am.

CHAPTER TWO
DIANA

It's been months since CiCi first told me about the proposal and we haven't heard a word since. When news of the king's death swept through the town, it was a shock to CiCi. My sister mourned the loss of being able to meet her future father-in-law and not being able to be there for her prince. But it didn't dampen her belief that the prince would return for her.

At least not until the morning she received the latest news from the prince's kingdom. Messengers were sent out from Roslani kingdom across the land. I see my sister crying, her shoulders heaving with the force of her tears as she watches the messengers leave. The prince is set to marry a princess from a neighboring kingdom. I watch as CiCi's eyes light up with hope. That is until we are informed that the wedding will take place in a year. CiCi did not make final plans with her prince, so this couldn't be about her. She is so upset by the news.

Despite being so distraught at the news, CiCi refuses to believe that it could be true. She has complete faith in the prince and his love for her. "It has to be something else. He wouldn't do this to me. Not without needing to. He loves me, Diana. He wouldn't do this. He just couldn't."

I watch over CiCi as the next few days pass, or maybe it's been weeks. I lost track when I noticed she was getting depressed. My days were filled with nothing but comforting my sister. From the morning meal to the evening meal, all she did was lounge about and talk about the prince she lost.

As I am about ready to throw my sister into the river and give her a wake up call, another messenger comes round, telling our father that Kellen, the prince, or is he now the king? Whatever he is, he is looking for some huntsmen. He wants these men to be there as a betrothal gift for his bride to be. He wants twelve of them, all ready to serve the well-being of his new bride to be.

Of course, our presence is ignored, but we inwardly digest every bit of this conversation. Our father is far too old to become a huntsman, and we don't have any brothers. So, he acknowledges the man's message and sighs when he turns to see us in the corner of the porch, having listened intently.

"What are you two doing here? Get back to knitting or sewing or cooking. That conversation was none for your ears." He shakes his head and heads off to tend the land again.

When I look back, CiCi's brow is furrowed, but she shakes her head when I ask her what she's thinking. Every now and then, she tilts her head from side to side as we cook our father some lunch. Little moments pass where she mumbles things I don't understand, but then she's back to stirring. I start to think my sister has lost her mind, then she shouts, "Aha!" as she raises the wooden spoon in the air.

I duck out of the line of sauce flying through the air and raise my eyebrows in curiosity. As she licks the hot sauce off of the spoon she just raised, not even noticing that she nearly splattered it all over me. "What is going on, CiCi?"

As though she's just noticed me, she looks my way. "I just had the most brilliant idea, sister."

I hate it when she calls me 'sister'. I don't feel like her sister. I feel like her brother. But she doesn't know that. I haven't gathered up the courage to tell her how I feel. But I keep these thoughts to myself as I roll my eyes and take the sauce spoon from her hand, putting it back on the stove. "What is this idea that you think you have?"

Her eyes widen as she puts out the heat from the stove. "Okay, hear me out. I want to go in as the huntsmen for the new bride of Kellen. I will be able to spy on both of them as a huntsman. Then I can find out what has caused Kellen to do this. There has to be something behind it all."

I look at her and shake my head from side to side. "You do remember that the man is looking for twelve huntsmen, right?"

She shrugs as she gets a glint in her eye. "Oh, I remember."

I shake my head as I sigh. "And you do remember the men part of huntsmen, right?"

Undeterred, she picks up the spoon she was stirring

with and smiles. "I think I have a fix for both issues. But I need your help, Diana. Will you help me become a huntsman for the new king?"

I find myself rolling my eyes at her, again. At this rate I'll make myself pass out from dizziness from rolling my eyes so much. "You really think you can pull all this off, CiCi? You really think we can all act as men, and learn to hunt? And how will we look like men. Surely, she will take one look at us and know we are women." She nods and I shake my head. "Fine, I will go along with your crazy scheme, since you seem to be dead set on it. What do you need me to do?"

After having served our father his supper, CiCi and I head out to meet a friend of hers. When we get to her house, she pulls both of us away from the entryway instead of inviting us inside.

"CiCi. What are you doing here?" the woman whispers as she looks around like someone might spot us.

"I need to know where to find the witch." CiCi whispers.

"Witch!" I shout.

The women glare as they shush me.

"CiCi, you didn't say anything about a witch," I whisper back.

CiCi just waves me off as she turns back to her friend. "I know I promised I wouldn't say anything, but this is important. I need to find ten other women and I need us all to become huntsmen."

"Huntsmen? For King Kellen?" she asks.

"Yes, it's a long story and I'll explain it to you another time. Just trust me that I know the risks..."

I stand in shock as my sister explains this crazy idea she'd concocted.

Not only does she plan to lie about an ability to hunt, but she plans to seek a witch's help in doing so. I feel like this may be a mistake, but knowing my sister, I won't get away with not helping her.

And just like me, CiCi's friend caves and spills the details about the witch's home, "There is a cottage deep in the woods. The witch lives there and she sells potions. I know they work, cause I myself have tried a few," explains her friend. Her eyes turn to me. "I think you should go with CiCi and grab the potions we need. She will turn us into men, in our outwardly appearance. Then we can get into the castle as the huntsmen they asked for."

I shake my head. "We are going to get caught. And what will our fathers say? Will we tell them we are going on a woman's retreat?"

CiCi smiles as she turns to me. "I really don't care what happens to us after or during this. I want to see what has stolen my prince's heart. He was mine, and I will get him back with you without your help, lovely sister."

I frown at the word lovely used in front of addressing me. Since we were children that word thrown out never meant what it really did. "Fine. I will help you, but you owe me so big, sis."

Her friend leaves, laughing as she walks away. "Have fun with the witch, she really is a character."

With that, I turn to leave, CiCi stops me, grabbing my arm. "She said the cabin is that way."

I shrug. "I was going to go home first?"

She doesn't buy it and drags me with her. "I will go with you, sister, and we will make sure we get all the right things." She shakes her head angrily. "If you can't even get the direction right then how can I trust you to remember what potions to get?"

I just look at my sister as we walk through the woods to a dark-looking cabin. I hesitate to go in, but CiCi drags me. I could pull away and be gone, but I find myself more curious about what this witch can do. *If she can make us appear as men, can she change us permanently into men?*

Before I know it, CiCi's hand is gently tapping at the door of this creepy cabin. The door opens and the witch, who has a sinister sort of beauty about her, smiles in CiCi's direction. "What can I do for a beauty such as yourself..."

Her eyes catch on me as she hesitates. "Uh, CiCi, my sister here, was engaged to the new king before his father fell ill. She wants to see him again, but the only way we can is if we act as his huntsmen. Is that something you can help us with?"

The witch doesn't seem to acknowledge the fact that I just asked her something. Her graceful way of changing the topic is so hard to keep up with. "What potions have you taken to make you this way?"

I tilt my head not sure what she's talking about. "I haven't taken anything. That's why we came here... to get something."

She squints her eyes as she steps out of her cabin,

pacing around me as she looks me up and down. "There's something off about you, child. Something that is hiding under the surface waiting to come out."

I find myself thinking about all the feelings I've had lately. The feeling that I am not a woman, for one. The witch's eyes keep exploring every inch of my womanly body. I can't help but think about how much I don't want to have this form. All I want is to be a man. Not that I would ever say as much to this witch. Who knows what powers she has? What hold she could have over me with that knowledge.

Luckily, my sister steps in, putting herself between the witch and me. "Don't worry about Diana." Her hand waves dismissively at me, as she continues, "She's not what is important. I need a potion that will make us appear as if we are men."

The witch reluctantly looks at CiCi, her head tilting to the side as she takes her request in. "Why do *you* need this?"

CiCi huffs in irritation, as the witch obviously missed what I had said earlier. "We want to become the prince's huntsmen. They wouldn't accept women as huntsmen, even though I'm sure Diana could beat any man out there at archery. Still, it's best to keep with the appearances."

The witch's eyes widen as she rubs her hands together. "Are you planning to assassinate the prince?"

CiCi shakes her head violently from side to side. "No!" The way she is looking anxiously at me has me shaking my head. I know that CiCi is going to crumble, so I get ahead of her. I don't want her to be a mess of depression again.

I smile, trying to get these potions the best way I know how. "We want to protect the prince, at all costs. He's a dear friend of ours, but because of these laws we can't watch out for him. That's why we want to appear as men, so we can be his huntsmen and guard him while he's newly crowned."

The witch looks at me quizzically, her eyes shining the longer she stares. "It's a lie. You're entire being is full of lies and half-truths. Have you felt it yet? The wrongness that festers within."

I suck in my breath at her words. I just know she's talking about my desire to be a man. I know that's the lie, the wrongness she is talking about.

I don't have to stew in it long, as CiCi pipes up, "Please! I love him. I love the prince and he loves me. See." She shows her hand to the witch, sighing as she says, "But something is stopping him from marrying me. That's why I know we have to go there and help. He couldn't be doing this of his own free will. Not after the promises he made to me."

The witch peers at CiCi, as though she is trying to see straight through her. "There's no falseness to you. I will help you win your prince. But you will owe me a favor, whatever I ask, you must give it to me," she finishes with a nod.

I look at CiCi, sighing as I take in all the witch is saying. "Don't. You don't know what it is she could want."

I watch as my sister makes likely the biggest mistake

of her life. "Nothing matters, if I can't be with Kellen. So, whatever I have to give up is worth it."

I find myself stepping in, before my sister can sacrifice herself. "No, I'll do it." My eyes meet those of the witch as I say, more firmly, "I'll take her place. If you want a favor, you can take it from me."

The witch eyes me again, circling me and looking closely into my eyes. I don't know what she is thinking, but I feel that it can't be anything good.

Her mind made up, the witch taps me on the shoulder, saying in a creepy tone, "Yes, you'll do. You'll do nicely."

CiCi tries to stop me again, but I tell her with a glance that she needs to shut up. "Just think of this as my wedding gift to you, sis."

We step back as the witch begins her spell. She's mixing various potions into her cauldron. At one point she steps over to me and gives me something to drink.

I take one look at the gross liquid, not sure what exactly she's put into it. "What is this?"

Rubbing her hands together, she smiles. "It's your favor to me." Tapping the side of the cup she handed me she adds, "Drink it, if you want me to complete the rest of the potion."

I take one more look at it, seeing something possibly human floating in it. I take a sniff of it and immediately regret it. This is going to taste so awful going down. I am almost ready to hand it back to the witch and abort the mission, when I look into my sister's hopeful eyes. Resolve established, I tip the cup back into my open mouth, swallowing down every last drop.

The witch smiles as she moves away from me, standing in front of the cauldron again. As she's moving, I feel something pulling at me. No, it feels more like it's attaching to me. I feel like this thing that's gotten ahold of me won't let go. Every nerve ending in my body starts to tingle and I can feel every second of it.

When the witch raises her hand, I'm jerked forward. I catch myself on the cauldron, as tendrils of magic cover me. There's a pulling over my whole body. It feels like something is being yanked from me and sucked back into the cauldron. As the final tendril is ripped from me, I go down on my knees in excruciating pain. Through the mind-numbing pain and terror, I hear my sister clear as day, "What did you do to her? Did you hurt my sister?"

It takes me a while to catch my breath, and to start feeling anything other than pain again. When I do finally feel like myself again, and my breath is coming and going easily, I look between the witch and my sister.

"I did what was desired," the witch answers as she moves over to me. Standing over me, she jerks my head up and pours more liquid into my mouth. It's even more vile than the last batch she forced on me and I don't know if I can take it down. The witch closes my mouth, then covers both my mouth and nose. With no choice I swallow it all down. The way it burns as it passes through my throat has me wanting to puke it up.

The witch's hold over my mouth has me gagging and grabbing at my throat. This is no normal burn of boiling liquid; this is more than that. The witch's eyes meet mine as she nods, seeming satisfied with my pain. "It's done."

The finality in her tone, followed by a harsh laugh, has me cowering down to the floor.

I can hear my sister asking, more calmly this time, "What's done? What did you do to my sister?"

"Your *sister* is about to get what they want." I glance up from my spot on the floor, still in agony, just in time to see the witch look at CiCi. "Which is to help you. Is it not?"

I run my hands over my body to see if anything changed. What else could she have meant when she said what I want? Besides helping my sister there wasn't anything else I wanted.

Unless... Did she have the ability to give me the body I wanted? Was she powerful enough to not only know my deepest secrets but to bring them to life?

The witch pours the potion into vials then hands them to CiCi as I try to stand up. "Have your huntsmen drink this, before going to the castle. It will give all of you the illusion of being a man." I watch as she grabs a hanging pouch of dried herbs, before adding, "Eat one leaf from these herbs, when you want to become your true self again. Be cautious. Once the spell is removed you won't be able to cast it again."

As my pulse settles and the queasy feeling churning in my gut stops turning I suddenly feel like I am no longer who I was before

CHAPTER THREE
NOT DIANA

I still can't do a whole lot, the way the potion has affected me, I need CiCi to lean on, the whole way home. Every step is still filled with pain. But I feel more me than I have ever felt before. After a long walk through the woods, I find myself collapsing onto my bed in our home. My body feels like it is overheating. The way the heat burns through me, I feel as though I will be cooked from the inside out. I may even turn to ashes, if this burning continues.

In my rare moments of consciousness, I feel the care from my sister and my father. I can tell they are doing everything they can to keep me alive. Between bouts of sleep and being awake, I can see their faces growing more and more concerned. I don't know how long I'm out for, or how much pain I've put them through, but, suddenly, I'm awake.

I try to move, but my body shifts differently than it used to. Sitting up in bed, the covers fall from my chest. The nightgown I've worn for years doesn't show any curves. Not that I used to have much that you could call curves before. How long have I been out that the heat of the fever took away all my muscle tissue? Am I an invalid now?

I move to get up, noting the way my muscles move. That I am much stronger than I used to be. That's not a normal side effect of being in bed for many days. When I walk towards the door to my room the top of the frame is closer than it used to be.

Significantly closer.

I'm still coming to grips with these changes when I make my way to the living area. There I see CiCi, and a group of women gathered round our kitchen table. When they notice me, I hear a collective gasp.

I look around the room, confused as to why they are all staring at me wide-eyed. "What's so surprising?"

I watch as my sister, her face still filled with shock, approaches me slowly. She stops in front of me. I have to bend my neck more than usual to meet her eyes. She put her hand on my chest.

. Her hands are on my chest, then slowly she moves one down each arm. My mouth opens on a gasp as I go to move her hands off me. "Are you out of your mind, CiCi? Why are you feeling me like this?" It's not like I was out for years. Maybe days, but not years. Why are you so surprised by me? And why do you keep touching me?"

CiCi puts a hand on either side of my face as she holds contact with my eyes. "You've only been in bed since yesterday."

This doesn't make sense. It felt like I'd been out for days. "Then that's even more reason to stop touching me. It's only been a day. You could catch whatever I had." I can feel the sass in my tone as I keep pushing her hands away from me.

CiCi looks at me in concern. "Diana, you don't understand." My sister grabs my arms and turns me until I am facing the mirror. Even through its distortion I can tell the person staring back at me is a stranger. "Look, you've changed completely."

It must be some trick in the mirror. It's a mean trick at that. Slowly, I walk closer to the mirror, looking for the truth behind the trick. As I find none, I reach for my face, at the same time, a man, staring back at me does so too.

Thinking this can't be so, I wave my arms around, frantically trying to trick the reflection in the mirror. Sure enough, the mirror man and I are moving at the same speed, doing the same things, and he looks more me than I have ever felt.

He has long, dark hair with sharp cheekbones just like mine. His face is longer with a more prominent jaw. But it's the eyes. My family have always said I have unique eyes. Not just hazel, but a hazel that shines like molten gold.

The man in the mirror has the same eyes.

Is this what I would have looked like if I'd been born in the right body?

My attention is drawn back to the silence in the room. I turn to CiCi and her friends, asking, "What?"

I watch as CiCi's face goes from concern, to outright happiness. She starts jumping up and down as she claps her hands. "It worked! I can't believe it worked."

I look around the room as the other women also

start to jump and clap their hands. I can tell they are excited to help CiCi, but I am just so unbelievably happy that it's as if an enormous weight has lifted off me and for the first time in my life, I feel like I am in the right skin.

CiCi looks around, making eye contact with me and each of the women. "Gather around, we need to figure out what our next steps will be, huntsmen..." She giggles at her own words.

I only spare half a mind to them discussing in the background all the logistics of this endeavor. I don't care about any of it. Whether CiCi gets her prince, or we come crawling back after a failed mission. Just having this moment of rightness is worth anything that happens next.

I love this body, from my chest lacking the fluffy lumps, to the bulge I can now see in my lower front. It's almost like the way I saw myself in my head has come to life. I feel like I can really be myself. I look and feel exactly as I had in my dreams. That makes me want to look underneath the hood, to see if that has really changed, or if I am imagining the lump there.

Out of nowhere, it feels, I hear my name, one that doesn't seem to fit me anymore, called out loud, "Diana!"

I can feel the blush on my cheeks as I turn around. They don't need to know the thoughts I had as I was looking at myself in the mirror. "Yes, CiCi."

Her eyes glisten with excitement as she says, "Come here. Now that we know the potion works, we need to get everyone ready for the attack on the castle."

I find myself nodding along, happy to do anything to

stay as I am, a man, in a man's body. When CiCi doesn't continue, I look at her, asking, "What is it?"

CiCi looks at me then twiddles her thumbs nervously as she says, "Well, I don't exactly know what needs to be done to be a huntsmen. But you know everything about those types of things... so maybe you could help us so we can do the same. The prince won't take us on if we can't actually hunt."

That makes perfect sense. I look around at the women looking to me for guidance. Each of them look as though they have held nothing sharper than a butter knife. I know for a fact none of these women have ever shot a bow or skinned a deer. I have so much work ahead of me, I don't know if I can manage it.

CiCi smiles an uncomfortable smile as she pats my knee. "Finally, all those unusual... *diversions*..." The way she says the word has me on edge, like I did something wrong by learning all these things. "Will come in handy for once."

I could feel my back tense up and had to look away from CiCi before she could see my feelings on my face. The way she dismissed my hobbies, making them sound less than everything she's done, really hurt me. Once I got the look on my face under control, I looked into CiCi's eyes, then at all of the other women who are now depending on me and my *diversions*, they hate so much.

My mind made up, I turn to them. "Well, to start, have any of you ever shot a bow?"

The way they all stare at me, their faces blank and their eyes empty, gives me my answer. Internally, I shake my head before asking, "What about riding a horse—"

One of CiCi's friends cuts in, "–Oh, I have! I love riding them."

I nod, a snarky smile on my face as I finish my sentence, "Astride?"

Her eyes widen as I raise my brow, having finished my sentence. "What?"

I tilt my head, smiling, trying to make this as easy as possible for them to understand. Waving my hand at her, I ask, "What's your name?"

She sits proudly, her shoulders only slightly slumped as she says, "Millie."

I nod, happy to know her name. "Millie, then, have you ridden a horse astride? Not side-saddle."

Millie's eyes lower to her lap in understanding. The defeat is evident on her face. She doesn't say another word, she just shakes her head.

I find myself nodding for their benefit. This is going to be a lot harder to do than I originally thought. Is it even possible to turn eleven women into huntsmen? That thought is dismissed from my mind as I realize I'll finally be able to spend my days doing something I love, instead of having to sneak off to complete it.

With a new energy growing inside of me, I clap my hands and look around the room as I rub my now manly hands together. "Okay. This is what we're going to do." My eyes travel around the room as I get ready to explain how the next few weeks will go. I need to get all of these women in fighting form, if we are ever going to pull this off. "We will start with archery. All of you need to know how to shoot an arrow into a deer's heart, so it doesn't suffer."

At their blank stares I start to sigh. CiCi chimes in, "Okay, I can do that."

Her friends follow her in agreement. If she can do it, so can they. I smile as I add, "When you have all perfected that, we will get started on another task."

The way they cheer for me helping them has me smiling. They won't be smiling long. It takes time to build up muscle enough to string a bow, pull it back, and then shoot it. They will hate me for teaching them this first, before the first week is done.

The knife skills they would have learned in the kitchen. If they didn't spend hours with a bow in their hands, they would never learn it. Since they are so anxious to learn, I grab my bow and some arrows, ready to teach them.

"Let's get going then. There is no use in wasting time, is there?"

All eleven of them stand up and follow me into the back yard where they will learn all they need to know to become an archer like me. The sound of their excitement hits my ears and I look around at them. I know they are just in this to help CiCi, but the fact that they want to know has me standing tall.

Standing in front of them I put a few arrows in my quiver, then set my stance ready to test out this masculine body against the old female body I once had. I feel each muscle work, the way they are meant to. I can feel the talent I already had growing as I shoot each arrow at the center. Having a man's body allows me to do what I have always wanted to do.

The women just watch me as I hit the target straight

in the middle, three times. I can feel their eyes on me as I head to the target, ready to explain how I did that.

The first one to say anything is my sister. "Was it just me, or did you do better as a man than you normally do as yourself?"

I shrug as I walk back having taken the arrows out of the target. "I feel like I have better control of my new muscles than I did of my old self." I shake my arms out, ready to get started on teaching instead of just showing. "Anyway, I want you all to start with your stance." I get into the right stance, showing them what to do. Each of them stands in the same way I am. "Good, now I need you each to hold one of the bows that are out here for practice. You need to get the feel of how heavy they are."

"I can't lift this," shouts one of the women.

"You can to, just hold it in your hands, up in front of you like this." I show them how to hold the bow when it's time to shoot. I hear them all moving, and when I turn around, I see many of them falling and fumbling. "Well, that's a start." I shake my head as the one who said she couldn't hold it, is actually holding it perfectly. "Now, without the arrow in there, just pull back on the string." I stand next to her to help her, if needed.

"Wow, that's a lot of pressure. I think I can do it though." She eyes me, like she is hoping she is doing it right.

"You will get it, now slowly release the tension, then pull back again, until it becomes as easy as slicing through butter."

Dutifully, she nods, getting to work and shining as she starts to allow herself to really learn. By the end of the first hour, all of them are holding their bows correctly, and controlling the pull back of the string. The next step is going to be much harder, and since it's nearing supper time, I decide I will head to bed.

"Okay, ladies, we are done for the night, let those muscles work and grow. When we wake up tomorrow, I will walk each of you through loading the arrow in the bow." I turn away from them and head back to the house shaking my head and mumbling, "Maybe you will even get to shooting one by the end of the day tomorrow."

None of them hear me as we head in and get supper ready. The day went on as usual, and I just fall into bed, completely exhausted with all that has happened so far.

The whole of next week is filled with teaching them how to work the bow, before even getting an arrow loaded. At the end of the week, I let them start shooting at the targets. The friend who was doing well on day one continues to shine, getting at least one arrow on the target on her turn.

I can't say the same for the rest of them. Each one of them misses, most barely make it to the same area as the target. There was one who almost hit one of the others when she turned to talk to me, instead of looking at her target. This is going to take a lot more than one week to get them all trained to be huntsmen.

At night I would teach them about hunting, the skinning, the killing, and the dragging. They really don't like getting messy, but they will have to learn to get messy, if they will ever succeed in this.

Another week goes by like it's nothing, each moment is used to the fullest as they learn. I find that at least half of them are hitting the target, even if it's not the middle. And a few of them are actually hitting the bullseye.

Adding in riding astride is the next step. I take them to the horses, smiling as I look around at them. "Are you all ready to learn to ride a horse like a man?"

The cheer that rises up would make the neighbors suspicious if we had any, that is. I shake my head as I see them all in dresses, still not having taken the potions. I on the other hand am wearing pants, they work so much better when riding astride.

I get up on the horse and smile when she bucks a little. She is my horse, so she is used to riding this way. I guide her by squeezing my legs at the right times in the right places. By the time I have made a full circle, all the women are staring at me.

I dismount my horse and hand the reins to CiCi. "Here, sis, you give it a try."

Her eyes widen as she looks down at her bulky dress. "In my dress?"

"Yes, sis, in your dress. Then maybe tomorrow you'll wear pants and ride even better."

She gets on the horse and starts to ride off, her legs falling in stride as she gets used to the feel of my mare between her legs instead of under her. After two rounds of the paddock, she stops the horse in front of me with a huge smile on her face.

"That was amazing!"

I just take the reins as she gets off, handing my mare to another of the women here. By the time they all had tried riding astride, my mare was worn out. I take her back to the stable and give her a rest. As I'm brushing her, the brave friend of CiCi's comes up behind me.

"Hey, it's really nice of you to teach us. I just have to say, you look so much happier since you've become a man." A giggle escapes her, and her cheeks turn red. "Have you uh... checked the equipment? Does it work?"

I know exactly what she's asking, and I have no patience to answer her question. "I guess you'll have to find out when you take on a man's body, now won't you."

Her face red, she takes off, not saying another word. I just shake my head as I talk to my mare, "Not even a full two weeks of this and they still have so much more to learn from me. I don't see this working, but I would gladly keep this man's body, equipment and all."

After putting the brush away and heading to the house, I run into CiCi. "Hey, Diana, what do you think about our progress?"

I suck in my breath at the name I'd heard thousands of times but had never felt like mine. I didn't want it anymore. But how do I get her to understand that without telling her the truth?

"Umm... I've been thinking," I pull her to the side close to the archery field we'd constructed. "You shouldn't call me Diana, anymore."

I huff a laugh to cover my nerves as I look at her. "Do I look like a Diana? Before we dive headfirst into this adventure of yours, we should be used to being called by something else, don't you think?"

She stares at me without saying a word, before she slowly nods. "You're right. We'll have everyone pick their name tonight. It should probably something similar to their own name, so it is easy to remember."

"That sounds best."

"Have you thought of your name?" she asks.

The question makes me pause. I hadn't, actually. Even though I'd known for years that I didn't feel right in the body of a woman I'd never stopped to think of what I would be called if things were different. So many names race through my mind. The enormity of the decision is overwhelming.

"You know, before Mama died, she told me she named you after the Goddess Diana. She said it was because your delivery was so difficult. You were early and didn't come out the right way."

"When did she say this?" I ask.

"When I asked her about babies. She told me what to expect."

I frown. "She never said anything to me about it."

CiCi smiles. "You weren't much interested in learning about babies."

I shrug, knowing she's right.

"Anyway, she said that your birth was hard on her and that the Goddess Diana must have been holding her hand through it all for you to survive. In honor of that she named you Diana, after the Goddess of childbirth."

CiC's smile turns gentle. "But you know, she's also the Goddess of the hunt as well. I think Hunter would fit with mother's wishes, too. Don't you think?"

I turn my head away and blink a couple of times to stop the stinging in my eyes. When I turn back to CiCi, I nod erratically, "Yeah, that's good." My voice is scratchy, so I clear my throat before turning away and answering her original question. "I think we need another good week or maybe two before we are ready."

The last week of training is going by quickly and they are learning at lightning speed. Having them all take the potion, so we are all in our male forms, really has helped them to grow. It took some time getting used to their new deep voices, but now we are on the right track to be in the running for huntsmen. I worked them all hard and made sure we got all the mannerisms down. Each of them wanted nothing more than to help my sister.

I only want to help my sister. The best way I know how to do that is to be the hardest teacher to them. The way I see it, at least one of us should have a happily ever after, when all is said and done. I just know that it won't be me. I will not be the one getting my happily ever after.

I really don't want CiCi's version of happily ever after, anyway.

I'm standing in the field watching as all these women who look like men cut apart the kills they just took down. CiCi comes up to me, in her new male form. "Do you think we're ready?"

"I think we should be good. Having this last week to practice in their male form will be beneficial. I know when I changed, my body didn't respond the same way anymore. But this should be enough for them to know what to do."

We watched them together, smiling as each of them have made a ton of progress. All this progress means nothing, if we don't get a chance to be in front of the new king.

I look over at CiCi. "So, what is your plan for getting us in front of the prince to offer our services?"

The smile she gives me tells me nothing and everything at the same time. Her eyes glisten as her male form of a face looks back at me. If I didn't know better, I would say she is planning a devil's scheme, for her face is devilish.

CHAPTER FOUR
LEO

I trail behind Prince Kellen as we work out horses through the thick foliage of the forest. My eyes don't stop as I scan the trees surrounding us. This new habit of his is becoming ridiculous. A person can't hide away in the forest, hunting imaginary animals just to avoid speaking to their people.

Yet, here we are again, traipsing through the forest without any huntsmen to assist him under the premise of refilling the coffers with meat for the winter. Only we never return with much of anything.

I can't blame him, though. The loss of a father is difficult to get past. But to lose his father the way he did, and with that damn deathbed promise making things even harder. It is understandable that the prince isn't ready to face the villagers. They don't know the truth, so their congratulations on his upcoming wedding is a stark reminder to the love he lost.

No matter how many times I tell him that if the king had known about his love, he wouldn't have asked what he did it doesn't change the fact that he made that promise.

It is disconcerting to both admire him for his loyalty to his word and curse him for it as well.

Not that any of it has anything to do with me. Who he marries won't affect my place in his life as his friend and master guard. Yet, I can't help but worry about my friend.

"Sire. Don't you think it's time we head back? We've been out here for a while."

He looks back at me, smiling. It's a fake smile, but a smile nonetheless. His eyes find mine as he goes to dismount his horse. "I don't feel like going back just yet, Leo."

As he's walking through the forest, kicking around leaves and really doing nothing, we hear a cry from deeper in the woods. We get back on our horses and rush over to the source of the sound.

As we break into a clearing, we see a woman rushing through the forest, chased by a man in a mask. She trips over her own feet and lands face down. We are too far away to reach her before the man. Despite that, we take off at a gallop, ready to defend this young lady and her honor.

From the tree line a group of men on horses break through, in pursuit of the man. I watch closely as they block the path of the man to the woman. They surround him

One of them breaks off the formation to ensure the woman is safe. Another steps forward squaring off against the attacker.

I watch the man, the one who is fighting the woman's attacker. He is bold and I love the way he stands up for the woman. I also love the way his muscles ripple and find myself growing a bit hard at the sight.

It's not long before we are in front of the huntsmen, ready to address the situation. The huntsman I was admiring from afar has the other man subdued. He's holding him tight, the man's arms behind his back as he twines them together.

Another one of the huntsmen sees them and stops them from crossing an invisible line. "I'm sorry, sir, please wait here, while we subdue the criminal."

I jump off my horse and make my way to block the huntsmen from Kellen. "Who are you and what are you doing here?"

Just as I finish my sentence, a third man comes up. This one has a look of dominance on his face. He must be the one in charge. His eyes are looking at me, then they travel to our new king. I can almost feel love in those eyes. He bows in front of Kellen.

Their clothes are worn and dirty, like they've been out in the elements for a while. Mud is crusted over their boots. There was rain in the north three days ago. Were these men there? "Your Majesty. I apologize for the spectacle here."

I shift to block the prince from both of the strangers. I won't bother drawing a weapon, since I am the weapon. There is something wrong with these huntsmen, but I just don't know what it is yet. The way my instincts are going off, I know for a fact that these are not ordinary huntsmen.

Looking back at Kellen, I can see that he is interested in the leader of these huntsmen. I know most of the men in this land, I don't remember ever seeing this man's face though.

I shake my head as I watch Kellen get off his horse and head in the direction of this man we don't know. "Stay back, Kellen." He of course ignores me, going around my body, the one made just to protect him, and facing this man.

I wait for my king to make a move, so I can make one too. "I believe my guard asked who you are." The way he is looking at this man's face has me questioning his sanity. He is far too close for me to save him if the man pulls out a dagger.

The man bows before Kellen, looking at me with a cursory glance. "We are the huntsmen of Arden. I am Commander Charles Pumpernickle. We have been in pursuit of this man for days now."

I get closer to Kellen, keeping a close eye on this new man. "What will you do with him?"

I see a bit of uncertainty cross the man's eyes as he says, "Me and uh... my men will escort him back to our town, for him to pay for his crimes."

Kellen looks between me and this man, his face a mess of confusion. "To Arden?"

Charles stands tall. "Yes."

I look at Kellen not sure where he's going with this yet. "Yet, you've been in pursuit of him for days?"

I think I can see where this line of questioning is going. Kellen is trying to trap them with their words. My eyes keep darting between my king and this new man,

Charles. Kellen's eyes soften as he speaks to Charles. I focus in on the stranger, not sure what I'm looking for. The more I look, the more I feel like there is something off with his face. I just can't put my finger on it though.

The man I was watching earlier, wrangling the attacker, approaches, looking at Charles. "Commander, he's ready."

I feel a jolt of something go through me at the sound of this man's voice. The way his voice is pulling me in has me looking between him and the king. It only takes me a moment to feel that this man's aura is different from the others he is traveling with. This man feels almost normal, as opposed to the others in his group. Something is just not right with them.

The commander nods and the huntsmen shift away. Kellen steps out, smiling as he asks, "Perhaps you might rest after your travels? It's always a pleasure to welcome such amazing huntsmen to our table."

The commander, who had already turned around and was ready to leave, makes a sharp turn back to Kellen. "It would be nice to eat something I didn't have to hunt for once."

The way this man looks at the prince has me concerned. He looks at him with more than casual interest. This wouldn't be the first time someone tried to insinuate themselves into the King's circle for nefarious reasons. But from the way Kellen seems to be just as interested in him, I don't know if he'll be in the mindset to listen to me any time soon.

I find myself standing there, watching Kellen follow the others. He walks his horse to the place where the huntsmen had left theirs. I let my eyes travel back to the huntsman who took down the attacker. If they are using magic of some kind, is he the one controlling it? He doesn't have the same aura around him the way the others do.

I keep following behind them, ready to step in at the first sign of trouble. I shake my head as I make my way to the crowd. I know they are hiding something, even if Kellen can't see it, I can. I will find out what it is they are hiding and when I do, I will expose them.

CHAPTER FIVE
HUNTER

My mind is a mix of emotions as we step into the large sitting room connected to the suite of rooms we've been given. As they all gather around, CiCi lets out a squeal that sounds off with the lowered tone to her voice. The others start joining in before I even shut the door behind us. The way they act like little girls is beyond wrong. They did this for a reason and if they keep this up, we are going to fail.

Done with it, I raise my hand. "Shush!" When they quiet down, I meet each of their eyes and shake my head. "Did you forget the reason we're here? What we've done to get to this point? You can't jump around like little girls anymore." I find CiCi's eyes and lock in. "You have to remember that you're acting as men now. Especially, with the prin-King's guard."

I pull my eyes from my sister, ready to wrangle them all in, as I have been doing for weeks now. I can see by the looks on their faces, that each of them is feeling the way they should after that outburst. I turn to my sister, ready to find out more. "Who is that person with the King? You didn't mention the guard."

The way she shrugs and rolls her eyes at me makes me angry. I can feel the testosterone building up in my body. "Well, of course, he'd have guards."

Going up to her, I grab her shoulders and make her focus on me. "You didn't mention one like that. He's more than just an average guard. The way he looked at us... it was like he could tell we had secrets to hide."

The heat I felt when that guard's eyes found mine. I could even feel him looking at me before they got to the scene. I am not only worried about getting caught, I am worried that something more will happen. My body did something, felt something when I brought the man to CiCi. I almost felt like I was on fire, wanting something. The way the man's eyes traveled my body, the way he stared at me, something was off about it.

I can hear the girly tone as CiCi says, "Diana—" I look at her and make a noise in my throat to remind her that we aren't our old names anymore. "Oh, right, Hunter's right. The guard did seem a lot closer to Kellen than I thought."

I look at her confused. "You don't remember him from when Kellen came to visit you?"

She raises her hands, offended as she says, "No! There was never anyone around." Then she puts her hands around her waist, folding them in a very female way. "I mean, I felt like someone might be there, but I never saw anyone. Kellen never mentioned any *one* guard in particular."

Wanting to get to the bottom of this, I pull CiCi's

hands away from her waist and ask, "What about a friend? A servant? Did he mention someone that traveled with him?"

I watch as she tries hard to keep her hands from touching her body, like women do when they are stressed. When her brow furrows up, she says, "He did mention he had a pet cat he liked to travel with."

Now my interest is peaked. "A cat?"

She shrugs and looks back at me. "That was it. I didn't even know he was a prince at first. I thought he was a knight or something from one of the neighboring towns. How was I supposed to know I needed to question him about things like this."

With as much information as I feel I can get from CiCi, I turn away and ignore their chatter. I knew there was something different about that guard. I just wish I could figure out what it was. Aside from the good feeling I had from that man's eyes on me, I had the same feeling that the witch gave me when she stared into my eyes.

It was a painful feeling, and it was even worse when she immediately ripped a part of me out. I can't help but wonder what the guard with the king may take from me. Would it be as painful, or as freeing as what the witch did?

The way I see it, the best thing I can do is to stay away from that man as much as possible. Nodding to myself in my head, I solidify the idea. I must stay away from that guard as much as possible. Who knows what that man can or wants to do to me?

The clap of CiCi's hands brings me back to the present. I look over at her and the others from my corner of the room. CiCi is already on her way to making some kind of decision. One I missed putting any input into.

"So, it's decided."

Having not heard a word they said while I was zoning, I look at CiCi. "What's decided?"

One of the other girls, the one who was showing the most promise in the hunter training gives me a look. "You weren't listening, were you?"

I shrug, trying to hide my embarrassment of not paying attention. "Of course, I was listening. You should know by now that I like running things through a second time, from the start to make sure we're all understand our parts."

The whole time I was training them how to be more like men, I would run the instructions once, then a second time. So, it was a great excuse. Now, the training was paying off, since I really wasn't paying attention. I could see that they were all accepting this excuse, so I leaned in, smiling as they repeated the plan.

The best student in the group went over the conversation they had just had without me. "So, we all decided that the biggest threat to the operation is that guard. And as the strongest of us, you should go and get as much information from him as you can."

The smile she gives as she finishes her sentence doesn't lessen the gravity of the situation. I had just decided I would stay as far away from him as possible, now my sister and her friends want me to go after him. How am I even supposed to go after him?

I put my hand up, stopping her from continuing, "You want me to go after the guard?"

CiCi smiles as she looks at me. "Not like to hurt or anything. And you'd obviously be no use at flirting. But, see if you could befriend him."

I raise my eyebrow and sigh. "Why?"

CiCi shuffles her feet from side to side, like a shy girl. "The more we know about this man the better our chances. He's the one thing we didn't plan for when we came up with this. If he's against us I know he'll poison Kellen's mind against me."

I don't want to do this part. So, I make a suggestion, "Why can't one of the others do it? I fought the criminal."

One of the others growl. "That 'criminal' was my cousin, Louis. You know he wasn't any match against you."

I scowl as I look at them. "He still got in some good kicks. My side aches every time I move thanks to him." I rub my side before making eye contact with them, one at a time. "And I didn't see any of you jumping in to help me."

Yet another one of them looks me in the eyes. "What did you say when we said we were sore and wanted to quit training?"

While another one finishes her sentence, "Deal with it and go."

Biting the inside of my cheek, I think, *I knew that training would come back to bite me.*

I fold my arms across my chest in a manly fashion, as I always have. This time though, the position fits the body. "Fine. What will you lot be doing while I'm gone?"

Yet another of them giggles as she says, "Helping CiCi get ready for dinner with her prince."

I roll my eyes at the way they are still acting like women. "Just remember, it can't be a dress."

I feel myself getting shoved out the door, to the sound of their laughter. When the door is closed, I hear no more laughter. Thank goodness for some sound proof room. They are not great at acting like men when they get excited.

I lean against the door, not sure what just happened in that room. I had almost full control until this very minute. I shake my head as I go to get up and head towards where I think the guard may be. Just as I start to walk away from the door, an image of the guard's eyes flash in my mind. I can't get those handsome eyes out of my mind.

With a shiver, I sigh. That's where it all went wrong. If I keep thinking of that man in such detail, I will never be able to help my sister achieve her goal. I need to focus on my job and get my sister her happily ever after.

CHAPTER SIX
LEO

T rush after Kellen as he makes his way to his room. On the way there, the amount of people bringing us to a stop to address him, is delaying my chance at discussing my concerns with him privately.

Alani, a young woman, and a maid, who is obviously using this moment to also flirt with the king, flutters her eyelashes as she says, "Sire, Cook asked me to tell you that the apples she received from the merchant were spoiled, so she won't be able to make a tart you like. Is there anything else you'd like?"

I can tell by the way she is talking she doesn't mean food. Her tone is very suggestive of her desires for the king. There is no point in her asking the king either question.

Kellen takes it in stride. "I'm sure whatever Cook decides will be fine for our guests."

Alani tilts her head to the side, smiling as she asks, "Guests?"

Kellen's eyes roll, he is growing impatient with this

one, I can tell. "Yes, we have huntsmen staying with us tonight." The way her eyes light up pisses me off. None of these men are really known, and wasn't she just flirting with Kellen? "Please make the others aware to make them comfortable. Oh, and, of course, let Cook know that we will have additional stomachs to fill."

I feel a growl growing in my throat as I say, "Sire, you can't mean—"

Just then a messenger comes up, sounding rushed and out of breath. "Sire, this notice came in from some of the townspeople they say that they've seen signs of animals in the forests nearby. They are concerned it might be wolves."

Kellen waves him off, not worried about it too much. "Tell them we'll look into it, and if there are wolves, we'll take care of it. Until then, they should stay inside at night."

Another messenger approaches, with what is sure to be a useless question. "Sire—"

Having reached my limit, I raise my voice and roar, doing everything in my power to protect my king. "Enough!"

Kellen pulls me towards a nearby room, saying to the most recent of an endless stream of messengers, "Don't worry, Cole, if it is something important you can speak to me before dinner."

Cole, not that I even knew his name, nods, showing his submission to the king. "Yes, Sire."

Kellen shoves me into the room, shutting the door behind us. He sighs and his face falls blank. It's clear he's drained, no one would see any of that when he was around the others. I know it's because of that woman from before. The one he would sneak out of the castle to see. He was always off visiting her, and he most definitely loves her. I look around while giving my friend a moment to get his bearings.

We are in the library, and the room is quiet. Well, except for the wood crackling in the fire, that is. I can tell by the look on his face he is angry. I don't care. I need to talk to him, to help him make better decisions.

After taking a few minutes to breathe, Kellen tilts his head while saying, "Was that really necessary?"

I stand tall, knowing that my roar was most necessary. "Yes. Very much so."

I watch my king go to a chair that's in front of the fire, plopping down hard on it. I step up to the liquor cart and pour him a drink. We're both quiet as I walk over to take a seat next to him.

Once I'm seated and comfortable with a drink in my king's hand, I ask, "Why can't you tell them to solve their own problems? Each of them should have known what to do. Yet they come to you. As if showing their ineptitude would somehow endear them to you."

The fact that he stays silent doesn't bother me. A brooding man is always a thinking man. I let him think as I gear up for the next round of important questions.

Having taken a drink, I look over at him. "Why did you let those huntsmen stay?"

Kellen slumps into the chair even more than he was a minute ago. "I don't know," he mutters.

I sit up straight, leaning towards him. "That's not an answer."

His shoulders slump and he looks at the fire, like he's lost to it. "Haven't you ever felt like something should be done. You don't know why, but the decision feels right to you."

I look at him, my voice dry and dull and my stare matching it. "No, never felt that."

He scoffs as he realizes how crazy his question was to someone of my caliber. "Right, I forgot who I was talking to. Though, I'm sure you can trust those stirrings are correct more than I can."

I know that he's talking about my ability. Not only do my animal instincts far exceed that of any other human, but my intuition is far beyond most human abilities. Kellen knows this, and that's why he is asking me this question. I can even feel the changes in the air before a single leaf begins to sway.

That doesn't mean that others can't feel what I do, they just usually feel it much less than I do. However, Kellen isn't in the best frame of mind at the moment. I can feel the two halves of him warring for top position. There is one side of him, still longing for the love he proposed to but left. And another side of him yearning to fulfill his duty to his kingdom, as well as his father's dying wish.

Still, I can hear him out and maybe he can shed some light on the feelings I'm getting from the group. I sit back in my chair, looking over at him as he continues to stare into the fire. "What is it you're sensing about this group?"

His eyes never leaving the fire burning in front of us,

he shakes his head. "I can't explain it. The Commander..."

After feeling what I felt, I am more curious as to what he has to say about the commander. "What about him?"

He shakes his head a second time and takes a sip of his drink. His words are whispered low as if he's almost talking to himself, "I'm probably just imagining it. But it feels like there's something there."

I pat him on the shoulder and sigh. "I understand. But, Kellen, there's something *wrong* about them."

Kellen looks at me, his eyes filled with curiosity. "Wrong?"

I scratch at my cheek, not sure what to tell him. I don't want to scare him, but I don't want him to think I am not looking out for his well-being, either. "I can't tell what it is exactly. The fact that you're becoming somehow entranced by them only adds to my thoughts that they could be using magic to fool you. What if they aren't huntsmen at all? What if they're something else?"

The wind picks up from outside and a creak sounds. I cock my ear towards the shelves filled with books. Just in case it's more than wind, I want to be able to hear it coming, a mile away.

Kellen, unaware of the wind picking up and the worry in my mind, continues, "You may be right. But then you may be wrong. I trust you'll figure out a way to learn the truth. You always do."

Kellen stands up, patting me on the arm as he sets his empty drink glass on the mantle of the fireplace. "I am off to more kingly duties. You stay here so you don't rip anyone's head off."

I snort as I watch him walk out the door. I hope he's not so clueless that he thinks I would rip anyone's head off, without good reason, of course.

When the door closes behind the king I stand. Quietly pacing the room, I keep my ears completely attuned to the slightest sound. Stepping past a dark row of books, I snap my arm out and grab something by the neck. When I pull him forward, I can see the fear in his eyes. I can sense the rate of his heart as he tries to get out of my grasp. Certainly, he knows the punishment for spying is nothing less than getting his head ripped off...

I smile as his eyes find mine. "Got you."

CHAPTER SEVEN
HUNTER

He's so close that he has to be able to feel my heart beating through my chest. Pinpricks of pain are around my neck where his fingers press in, but they are so sharp. Did he put a knife to my throat that I didn't see?

I dig my nails into his hand enough to loosen his grip. Then I sink my teeth into the soft flesh between his thumb and forefinger. He yanks his hand out of my mouth, but it's enough time for me to flee.

Quickly, almost too quickly to be human, he tackles me to the ground. I twist, landing on my back to scramble away, but he's too heavy to push away. His large hands grab my wrists and hold them to the wooden floor above my head.

With his other hand he grabs my chin and forces me to face him. "Who the hell are you?"

His hot breath hits my cheeks as he roars these words. But what stills my heart is when his pupils lengthen until their ovals and his irises turn a honey gold. That is something unhuman. I don't know what to do with that. The fear, and I'm not sure what else it is, have me so transfixed on his eyes that I forget what he asked me.

He harshly shakes my head before leaning in close. Suddenly, I remember what he had asked me. He wants my name. I don't know what good a name does when it looks like he's ready to kill me... "Hunt... Hunter."

His demeanor changes slightly as he laughs. "Hunter? A huntsmen named Hunter. That is either highly ironic, or your parents didn't have many aspirations for you."

My eyes round and I shoot back, "I like my name!"

Of course I would, it is a homage to my mother. It may not have been very imaginative but whoever thinks they'd have to come up with a new name. Yet he is right. It is what I aspired to. To be able to hunt and ride and fight, without the fear of being labeled a freak.

Even with his negative words, it is a thrill to hear someone call me by the name I want. A name that reminds me of the body I have. The body that I have always wanted.

It doesn't take me long to realize that I, and this body I am now in, are sprawled on the floor. The way this beast of a guard between my legs has me feeling, I know I'm going to blush. I can feel it starting in my cheeks, then shifting down my face as I move my body. I don't think about moving, I just do, to accommodate for the growing problem I have now that there is a guard between my legs.

I can feel my breath catch as my gut twists. The

feeling of our groins rubbing together is something I had been desiring since the first time I got into this body. The sharp feel of them grinding against each other, both solid and ready, wasn't painful. I could tell by his face that he's feeling it as much as I am. I watch his face closely as a muscle moves in his cheek, then his grip on my jaw tightens.

He looks like he's holding back as he licks his dry lips. "What were you doing spying in here?"

I struggle against him, once again rubbing our bodies together. "I- I wasn't spying! I just came to look at the books."

The tilt of his head has me getting harder as he slides his hand back down to my neck. "Then why didn't you make yourself known when we entered the room."

I kept my eyes on his, it wasn't hard to do, with how much they had changed and how much they just pulled me in, from the first time I saw him, even. If I dropped my gaze, he would know I was lying.

Swallowing hard, I answer him, "I didn't notice at first. By the time I realized, I thought interrupting would only anger you."

The low growl of a chuckle that comes out of his mouth has my bulge growing under him. "How'd that work out for you?"

Grinding my teeth, I take in his smug response. I didn't mean to get caught, and I was spying, for sure. But I can't tell him that, now, can I?

I make sure to show real anger in my response to him. "It was working fine, until you decided to attack me for trying to read a book. Who are you? You were with the king earlier today, weren't you? Then you should know I'm an invited guest."

Moving my arms, trying to get them away from him, I groan. When that fails, I put a smile on my face and jerk my hips up, again trying to flip the situation. There is no way I am stronger than this man. My attempt to do so is so short...

This man with yellow eyes tsks. Yes, he is more muscle than I could ever dream of having, and yet he tsks. "Invited, yes. Guest? I don't think I'd go that far just yet."

I watch as he shifts, letting me go and standing up to his full height. As I lay on the floor watching him stand up, all I can think of is how giant he looks, with his broad, thick shoulders. The long blond hair he has is thicker than any I have ever seen before.

Still standing over me, I can see his bulge, the evidence that I did to him what he does to me. Shaking his head he says, "I don't trust you. And if you have any ulterior motives I will find out."

I could feel my heart going miles faster than it ever should. It doesn't slow one bit, not until I see him leave the room and close the door behind him. I still don't move. The way he took me down like I was a sack of potatoes has me not wanting to move. That bulge in my pants is starting to go away, before I finally pull myself up from the floor.

I make my way back to the others, the whole way I am thinking about what it is that is different about him.

Why was he so able to take me down? Why did I get so engorged with him? I don't know where this adventure is going, but I am happy I came with her to try and keep my sister safe. Try being the operative word.

CHAPTER EIGHT
LEO

I step into the dining hall before supper is about to start in hopes of talking to Kellen. The fact that these huntsmen are skulking around in the rooms, listening in on conversations is proof that something needs to be done about them.

But when I enter the hall, he is not there. He's almost always here because he likes to show up early so, he can speak to any of his visitors or any advisors he didn't reach out to during the day.

I notice the maid from earlier today setting up the table. I make my way over to her, using my ability to tread lightly to stay quiet.

When I get to her side, I lean close and whisper, "Where is the king?"

Alani is startled by my sudden approach and puts her hand on her chest as she says, "Oh! Apologies, sir. His Majesty has not shown up for supper, yet."

I just lean closer, knowing she knows where he is.

"Why hasn't he shown up? Has he come down with some kind of sickness?"

Alani looks around the room, suspiciously. Her eyes drift to the side as she says, "No, sir. I believe he was meeting with one of the huntsmen."

The way my heartbeat picks up at the mention of them has me on edge. "Huntsman?"

Her eyes widen when she nods. I can tell she is afraid of me, a lot of the staff are. "Yes, sir. I saw him with the commander before meeting with Cook."

I click my teeth in annoyance, storming out of the room, intent on finding the king. They are in some other room. Just the king and the commander. The two of them are walking around the perimeter of the room. But that isn't what is the oddest.

The King has a smile on his face. I find myself smiling at the happiness that seems to radiate off him. I hadn't seen him smile like that in months.

I go up to him, putting on my professional hat, smiling and telling him, "Sire, it's time for supper."

Oddly enough, when he hears my voice, the smile disappears from his face. Why would his best friend and confidant's voice take away his smile? I stand there, still ready to escort him to the kitchen.

The commander looks over at me as if I were interrupting something important. I don't look away from their stare. Just as it did earlier, the longer I look into the man's eyes, the more a haze goes over them. The way his eyes hold mine, it is almost as if I was looking at him through a frosted window. I can make out all of his features, but there is a fuzziness to them all. His eyes are locked on me, and I am far from ready to lose his gaze, when I say, "Sire." I wave my hand towards the hall. It is only right that he lead the way.

His firm nod finds me first, then the commander, before he leads the way out of the room that he was just pacing with this complete stranger. The commander goes to follow, but I step in his path, wanting to make sure he is aware he won't get away with anything.

"I don't know what you're after, but if you have any ill will towards. The king I. Will. Find. Out. And *you* will pay."

I watch as the fear comes over the man's face. His eyes widen and his pupils dilatate, but not before I see the whites of his eyes clearly displayed. He takes a step back, fearing me. I breathe in the smell of his fear as he steps back.

My brows furrow the longer I stare at him. The fear I smell, the fear this man shows... neither matches with the man himself. The way he backed up from my intimidation really didn't seem like a man who commands a group of strong hunters.

"Commander," a voice behind me says. This voice sounds more like that of a commander, it's both firm and strong. The Huntsman from the library steps forward. The way he walks, and the way his body moves with authority, tells me this is much more of a commander than any other. As I watch him standing next to his commander, I can't help the way my body reacts to him.

Now, this is someone who can take charge of a whole army of men. Not that our kingdom needs a whole army, with me as our king's protector. A little assistance would be nice though.

Hunter, such a nice name, despite all the hate I gave him for it earlier, looks at the commander. The two of them seem to be talking with each other without saying a word. I don't understand it at all, but when he looks at me, I put my guard up. Still looking at his commander, he says, "Is there anything else you need, sir?"

From low in my chest comes a growl, as I say, "No." Leaving, with a quick turn back towards the dining hall, I shake off the feeling I get from Hunter. I may just be falling for his name alone.

Looking around the dining room, I see that the remaining huntsman have set the tables. The king is sitting at the head of the table in his usual place. I smile and take my place next to him as I get ready to eat my fill.

The rest of the dinner goes on as to be expected, that is until the end of the meal. I have yet to learn all the huntsman's names, but each of them seems to have endless questions...

One of them looks around the room and smiles as they make eye contact with Kellen. "I must say, your Majesty, your castle is beautiful. Has your future bride seen it yet?"

The man, if you can call him that, jumps quickly as if startled. A glare passes between this huntsman and Hunter. I find it interesting that Hunter seems to take more control of the conversation than his own commander. I wonder what else Hunter doesn't want discussed?

As if to clear the air, the commander clears his throat.

"Yes, we'd heard that you're soon to be married. You must be very excited."

I watch as Kellen takes a large sip from his wine glass. I know he has been wanting to avoid this topic the whole time. "I must," he says, smiling.

His lips are pulled tight and the joy one would expect to see on a newly betrothed man's face is absent. His eyes are filled with a sadness I am fully aware of, despite his not wanting to talk about it at all.

The feeling of the tension in the room elevates as the huntsmen all wait, their eyes on Kellen. I notice that their eyes keep bobbing between Kellen and their own commander. It's almost like they expect the king to fall for their commander, but he doesn't favor men…

A throat clears, as a voice I know all too well already says, "I spoke with some of your subjects as I was touring the castle and heard that you currently do not have any huntsmen in your employ."

My eyes move to Hunter as his voice echoes in my mind. I can tell where this whole conversation is going. Yes, we did put out a call for huntsmen to join us. However, we haven't had any really worthwhile men come up to the plate.

"Yes, we haven't had any in quite some time. After my father passed I hadn't the energy to search for new huntsmen," Kellen's voice is sad and downtrodden.

I watch as a look passes between Hunter and his commander. It's not long after that that the commander says, "Perhaps you won't mind if we stay longer, then. As we've captured the criminal we were chasing, we are currently without a task to complete."

"That is not—" I start to say, but I know that I won't be able to get a word in. Kellen seems entranced by this commander.

"Yes," the king says, cutting me off, just as I had expected him to. "That would be good."

"Sire—" My words are cut off with just one look from the King.

I can feel the growl rumbling up in my chest again. From the looks of the others at the table I know my eyes have changed. Quickly, I get to my feet and bow to Kellen. "Sire, if I may take my leave."

I only receive a curt nod, but that is all I need to know that I am now dismissed. Kellen knows where I'm going. I need to get out of here before something happens that I can't control. As soon as I leave the dining hall, I make myself walk faster, until I am almost running out the castle door.

I keep going until I get to the woods, I need to be outside the castle grounds in order to let my emotions out. I am a very emotional being and am heavily attuned to not only my emotions, but the king's as well.

When I reach the woods, I strip myself of the confining uniform and let go of my control. My bones shift and snap until I am in my true form. I toss my head back, my mane catching the night breeze as I let loose a trembling roar. It has me feeling only a little better, but I keep doing it until I am left with little anger.

CHAPTER NINE
HUNTER

Even in their deeper tones, the echoes of giggles are enough to have me rolling my eyes.

"Don't you think the king paid special attention to CiCi?" I groan as I hear Millie sigh the words.

"Yes," Emmalynn returns her sigh. "It's like you are destined for each other, proving he will love you no matter what form you take."

When I hear them, they all start to sigh, sounding more and more girl-like with each one, I get to my feet. They all startle with my movement. Which makes me happy, since they are all now silent.

I look around the room, feeling uncomfortable as I try to find the words to say what I am planning to do. "I-I should probably check on the others guarding our prisoner."

"Why?" CiCi asks, her eyes filled with genuine confusion, "It's not like Louis will escape."

My deep, new manly laugh fills the air as I try again, "Right. What I really meant is I'll see what I can find out about the guard, since we wouldn't want him spoiling our plans. But if he asks, I'll say I'm checking on our prisoner."

They all shrug off my flimsy excuse and go back to chatting. The conversation is of course the wedding plans that are always the goal for CiCi. I sigh as I close the door behind me, mumbling, "That was too much for me."

Being on the other side of the door still isn't enough distance between me and my sister's gaggle of friends. I find myself wandering through the castle. I make sure to follow the path that I remember, at least until I reach the courtyard.

I find myself asking a villager the way outside of the walls. They point the way and I make a run for it. I need to get away from all those women pretending to be men. I'm not pretending, since I have always felt as though I am truly a man at heart.

The way the sun glows against the horizon, only makes me want to get out of the walls quicker. I am only escaping for a short time. There is no way I will be able to escape the wrath of CiCi forever, but for now I can get away from the chatter of their female brains.

I love the way my muscles, building with power, eat up the distance between the castle and the surrounding forest. It's like an addiction the way the adrenaline courses through my veins. I can feel my heart beating wildly, the excitement and effort of the action spurring me on.

I find myself getting so lost in running, that I lose track of time, and space itself. That is, until I stumble over a branch. Looking around me, I take in the low lighting of the forest around me.

Down on one knee, still catching the breath I was losing, I start to really think about what could be out here. Feeling as though I have caught my breath, I straighten up. Suddenly, a wave of dizziness takes over. I shake my head, thinking it will make it go away. It has the opposite effect, and I find myself struggling to stay balanced.

I put my foot back to try and regain my balance. This also backfires when I hook my foot onto the same damn branch that tripped me up in the first place.

I hear my own cry echoing through the woods as I fall back down, this time not finding any footing and landing straight on my back. I listen as my voice is carried further than it would be in the day, silencing all the creatures near me.

I can feel my nerves tweaking as I wait for the life to come back to the forest. The silence is too much for me to bear, but I wait, lying flat on my back as I hear the woods start to come alive. I take a deep breath as I get into a sitting position, ready to stand up.

Happy with the noise going on around me, I make my effort to stand. The second I put pressure on my foot, a jolt of searing pain runs up my calf. Again, I scream, letting my pain show in the voice I let out into the world.

Silence.

Was this going to go on all night?

I get back on my ass, ready to look at the ankle I have apparently injured. This has to be the dumbest thing I'd ever done. I shake my head at the thought. No, the dumbest thing I did was agreeing to this insane plan of CiCi's to begin with. The pain I am going through now is just the aftereffects of the original stupidity.

I look around the woods, seeing only trees and hearing the wildlife starting to make noise again. Now, I'll be stuck in what would soon be a dark, creepy forest all night, with only a hope and a prayer that I don't get eaten by some forest animal.

I can feel the tears going down my face as I sit there, waiting for my death. After what feels like forever, I feel the hairs on the back of my neck stand on end. Freeze. That's what I need to do.

I stay still, holding even my breath as I try to keep from letting the pain and misery get to me. I listen to the woods around me, hoping there will be a sign before a predator hops out of the woods to eat me.

Nothing.

No, I mean nothing.

There is again no sound as I sit there on the ground nursing my sprained ankle. No sound. The same kind of quiet you get when there is a predator in the woods. All the animals go quiet in an attempt to evade the predator.

I take a shallow breath as I look ahead of me, into the woods. What I see gives me chills. Two gold orbs are peering at me from deep within the forest. I hope to God that they are just very steady fire flies. But that is unlikely. Especially since the two of them are moving closer to me. As they keep a steady pace in coming towards me, I notice some yellowish brown hair and a large tuft of it right around the neck.

I find myself scrambling to my feet, not thinking,

only to crash to the ground when I feel the pain in my ankle. The pain is bad enough that my ankle just lets me crash to the ground.

"What are you doing?" a deep voice asks behind me, a voice I recognize.

I whip my head around, looking to where only seconds ago a lion was standing, ready to feast on me. What I see when I look back at him is not only surprising, it's arousing. There, right before my eyes stands the king's guard, in all his naked glory.

Now, I have seen myself naked in this form and I have to admit I love it. That said, I love seeing his body way more than seeing my own, and in a much different way. He acts like he's not naked, coming up to me and grabbing my ankle.

"Your ankle should be fine in a day or so, but you won't be able to walk back to the castle yourself."

CHAPTER TEN
LEO

I go out into the woods to get away from all the mess at the castle. I feel off, so I run, and shift into my Lion form as quickly as I can. After running for what feels like hours, I hear a scream, or is it a shout, in the forest.

As suspicious as I am about these huntsmen, I start to rush over to the scream. I need to find out what it is. I find a man, not just any man, the huntsman who was in the library. He has screamed twice now.

Is that tears I see in his eyes? My night vision confirms that's what it is. He stops sniffling as he realizes that the forest is quiet, largely due to me being here. I smile as much as a lion can, happy to put fear into the things around me.

The man sees my lion form coming out of the trees and attempts to get up to scramble away from me. Not that he could outrun me on a good day, this time I see him stumbling before screaming again.

I just roll my eyes as I shift back to my human form,

not caring about my lack of clothes. "What are you doing?"

I grind my teeth to keep from snapping at the man. But the way he stares at me is causing my own body to react. I can feel myself growing under his heavy gaze.

Attempting to break the tension, I say, "Your ankle should be fine in a day or so, but you won't be able to walk back to the castle yourself." I don't want to say these next words, but there is no other option. "You can ride on my back."

"Your back?" Hunter looks confused as he looks at my chest, as if judging my words.

Internally rolling my eyes, I try not to take offence at the doubt in his eyes. We both know that I am strong enough to subdue him with just one arm. He isn't wrong about my ability to carry him on my back all the way back to the castle in this form, though.

He's already seen my lion form, it's too late to hide it now. "In my other form; my lion. I can carry you on my back in that form. Now, hurry up before it's completely dark." I step closer and he shifts back in fear.

"I don't have time to play with you like this," I say, tilting my head to the side like I'm talking to a child.

"How are you going to get us back in the dark? Shouldn't we camp here for the night." Not only can I feel the fear coming off him, but I can hear it in his voice too.

"I can see in the dark better in my animal form. It won't be a problem getting back, *if* you ever get to work," I say as I crouch down in front of him.

I wait for Hunter to get on my back, only when I feel his hand start to reach for my shoulder do I settle in. I find myself shifting uncomfortably as I feel something hard and long digging into my back. I assume it's his dagger. I groan in my throat when I realize that the dagger I'm feeling is actually the man's cock.

I shift without warning, and the man lands on top of me with a cry of alarm. I shrug him off.

He looks at me in shock. "What- Why did you do that?"

I raise my eyebrow at him as I shake. "I didn't feel like having you rutting against my back all night."

"What do you mean?" The confusion in his eyes has me wondering about him.

"Don't pretend you don't know. I felt it every time you moved." I look down at his cock as he stands there, still baffled.

"Felt what?" Hunter looks genuinely confused.

I reach out, intent on making this man realize that being aroused as he gets a ride back to the castle is not gonna fly. "This!" I shout as I hold on to him, making my point known.

Hunter's moan makes my cock twitch as I find myself not letting go of his cock. His moan is followed by, "But, but yours is the same."

I close my eyes not wanting to think of my rock-hard cock just yet. I don't want him to know that he is partly to blame for my situation.

I take my hand from his bulge as I sigh. "That's different. I'm not the one on your back, now am I?" I should curse myself for the words that are about to come out of my mouth, yet the second the image forms in my mind I can't stop them. "You should take care of that, now, then we can leave."

The way his face scrunches up, I would think he has never done it... Taking care of himself, I mean. "Take care of it?"

I find myself getting frustrated with him. "Yes! You need to get rid of it, before I'll let you near me."

The way this man looks down at his lap, as if he is still confused, has me losing my temper. I reach down to my own cock, gripping it and stroking it once. "Jerk. Off. Ya know, like this."

Hunter still looks confused as he says, "Um..."

I look at this man like he has two heads, there's no way he hasn't jerked off in his whole adult life. He has to be well past adulthood. "Have you never pleasured yourself before?"

With how quickly he answers while looking away from me, I already have my answer. "Of course I have."

The hitch in his voice calls him a liar.

I can feel my voice growing husky at the thought of teaching this grown man how to jerk off. "Take out your cock."

Hunter gasps at how blunt I'm being.

I stare at him sternly asking, "Do you want me to do it for you?"

He turns away from me and shouts, "No!"

I smirk at his reluctance to take care of himself. "Then undo your pants and take it out."

I know it isn't meant to be sexy, but the way he fumbles with getting his pants down, like it is foreign to him, turns me on. And when his cock is revealed, my mouth waters.

I move closer to him, and he freezes.

His eyes meet mine as he attempts to maneuver his cock. "What are you doing?"

What was I doing? "You won't be able to see what to do, if I'm far away."

Hunter nods his head, letting me know that he's okay with this move. I grab my cock and make one slow stroke, from tip to base.

Looking up into his eyes, I say, "Now you do it."

I watch closely as this man wraps his hand around his cock, a moan of surprise and pleasure going through him. I move even closer, but he doesn't seem to notice. His eyes close, shutting tightly as he moves his hand down his length. Only then does he look to me, his eyelids heavy.

His voice is barely a moan as he says, "Did I do it right?"

I find myself loving watching him, nodding my head I say, "Better but you need to keep doing it until you cum."

Again, I am faced with the confused glare of a man who hasn't handled himself yet. "Cum?"

I have to fight hard to hold back the laugh that wants to tumble out of me. "Trust me, you'll know when it happens."

Hunter gives me a shaky nod and makes another pass down his length. His movements match mine, stroke for stroke. "Sir?"

I keep my eyes on his cock as he keeps going, stroking

his cock and copying me. "That's right. That's perfect. Keep moving. Now see that, coming out of your hole. That means you're doing it right."

I watch as he nods, still very distracted by the new sensation. When he looks down and over at my cock, he smiles, then whispers, "Is yours doing it?"

I can't bring myself to use words, right now, so I just moan, letting the sound hang in the air. I pass my thumb over the tip of my cock, groaning as I do.

Hunter copies me, moving his thumb over the leaky tip of his cock. The way he gasps before falling onto his back on the ground, has me losing a bit of control too. It's then that I watch him writhing beneath me. Only then, do I realize that I'd shifted as he fell, to straddle him. I lean forward until our hands brush each other. The way he is gasping only spurs me on.

His eyes widen and he looks scared. "Sir? Sir? Something's wrong."

I smile as I watch him writhe on the ground, enjoying the approach of his first orgasm. Pushing his hand away, I add, "Nothing's wrong, Hunter. Just feel it." I take both of our cocks in my one hand, noting that the two of them fit perfectly in it.

The way Hunter grips my arms, I know his entire being is lost to the pleasure I am giving him. When he gasps, I swoop in, plunging my tongue into his mouth. His moans turn to whimpers, and I know he is close, just as I am.

I pick up the speed, thrusting into my hand against his cock, imagining it is going into his wet heat instead. His lips tear from mine as he cries out, sending us both over the edge. I feel myself collapsing onto him, smiling as I leave my hand firmly wrapped around both our cocks.

I'm supposed to be watching out for my king, not out here fucking the huntsmen. That said, this man really does it for me. There is a mess of cum between us, and I know we have to clean this up. Just as that thought hits me, I feel him start to come out of his haze.

I guess I better get off him and get ready to take him back to the castle. Sex can't cure an injured ankle.

CHAPTER ELEVEN
HUNTER

My lungs are on fire. The thoughts going through my mind at the sensations I just had with this man, the one who always seems to make my cock hard, are overwhelming. Yet, I feel like my mind is quiet and still. Even as a woman I had never taken pleasure like this. I didn't know until just now that this feeling was even possible.

I open my eyes slowly, feeling my heart slow down. The man above me looks shocked, yet satisfied as he hovers over me, his hand still gripping our cocks. Like a dam bursting, the moment our eyes connect every anxious thought slams into my mind. I open my mouth to speak, but nothing comes out.

Before I'm able to get my bearings, he climbs off of me and shifts. I scramble backwards. The beast before me is massive. Even as I sit on the ground, he towers over me. Did this man, who is actually a lion, just take my virginity?

I feel disheveled, getting to my feet I move to right

my clothes. That's when I feel something wet and slimy sliding down my stomach. Lifting my shirt, I brush my fingers over the thick liquid. I look up at the lion man, the king's guard, and now the guide to all things I now know about my penis asking a silent question.

I take a sharp breath in as the lion steps towards me. Shuffling back, I forget once again about my hurt ankle. I still try to get away from this man, or beast, or whatever he is.

He follows me until he gets me backed up against a tree. If lions could smile, I would bet that this is what it would look like, especially once I realize I am trapped. I hold my hand out, knowing it can't actually keep him away. My eyes close as I look away from him.

When a large wet tongue passes over my hand, my eyes shoot open. The beast is staring back at me without breaking contact, as he licks my hand clean.

His nose nudges the hand holding my shirt up, and I push it further up. My insides flip as he laps at my stomach, his eyes still locked onto mine. I couldn't look away, even if I wanted to.

"That-that was." I look down at my stomach. Then rush to right my clothes. "Th-thanks."

I hear a sound coming from deep within this beast that just licked my hand and my belly clean. It almost sounds like the purr of a cat.

Did he just purr?

No, it couldn't be. It was probably a growl, since I was taking too long.

I hold on tight as I ride this lion's back all the way to the castle. He lets me down close to the wall of the castle.

The Lion disappears, and I head in as quickly as I can. It takes a lot longer to get to CiCi with this limp, than it took me to get out into the woods earlier. When I get in there, the women are still in full bridal fever mode. I do my best to hide the fact that I hurt my ankle, by sitting next to CiCi on the bed.

I find myself listening, but barely, to the women masquerading as men. The other half of my mind is still processing what happened out in the woods. Was this a test to see if we really were huntsmen? Did what happened mean I passed, or did I fail?

One of the other huntsmen mention something that grabs my attention.

Laticia giggles. "I bet it will be just as beautiful as Princess Olivia and Prince Johnathon from Septillion kingdom. My mom talked about their wedding for years."

Jamilia looks around at the others. "I would think it'd have to be extravagant to make up for the rumors surrounding the prince and his advisor."

My curiosity gets the best of me when Jamilia says that. "What do you mean?"

Sitting beside me, CiCi says, "Oh, Jamilia, don't say that. You shouldn't spread gossip. Besides, they had two children so it couldn't have been true."

Iona leans in, making sure to get her two cents in. "But their children looked an awful lot like the Princess' head guard. More so than they did the prince."

I watch as CiCi winces, as if she can't refute that fact. But what could possibly have gone on between the prince and his advisor that would cause this gossip?

From the way they talk it is as if he had an affair, yet most advisors are men so that doesn't make any sense.

Unless...

I look around at the others who are already moving on to the next scandalous match between royals. I shift closer to CiCi and nudge her to get her attention.

I lean in close, whispering, "Was the prince's advisor a woman?"

CiCi sounds confused, but her voice is clean as she says, "Of course not."

I shush her as I look around, but no one had noticed CiCi's exclamation. Understanding quickly, she leans closer and lowers her voice. "You know advisors to the royal families are always men. Even the princess would have had a male advisor when she became queen."

I tilt my head as I try to wrap my mind around this whole thing. "Then the scandal was that the prince...?"

CiCi finishes my thought, "Was romantic with another man."

I nod, hesitating to ask her my next question, but need to know how she feels about this. "Do you think it's possible that two people of the same sex could love each other?"

I wait anxiously as CiCi pauses for a moment. My heart is in my throat, thinking that she may be against something that feels so big to me.

"I think love is such an amazing feeling, that sharing it with anyone must be a blessing."

I give her a slight smile. Before she can turn away, I touch her arm to get her attention. "What about someone not feeling like who they are? Like... a woman who wasn't really a woman. As if they were born in the wrong body for who they are?"

The way her eyes widen, make me feel like I may have gone a stretch too far with this one. When they sharpen and land on me, my eyes fall to my lap. I rub the palm of the hand the lion had licked, with my thumb. She takes so long to answer, that I worry I have offended her. But when I finally have the courage to meet her eyes, she smiles.

"I think anything is possible. There are witches and fairies and shifters all around us. People we would never know could be something so much more than what they appear. So, of course, it's possible that man or woman could be born in the wrong body."

My eyes well and I look away to keep the tears that want to fall inside. When I get better control of the turbulent emotions coursing through me, I turn back.

"Yes, of course," I reply as I give a quick nod. "Of course."

CHAPTER TWELVE
LEO

I find myself pacing in the practice area, watching closely as soldiers get the yard ready for archery. Kellen had stopped me this morning after breakfast to tell me his was thinking of having the huntsmen sign on in his employ. I tried many way to get him to reconsider his decision. Not a single one of them had any effect on his plans. It seems as though he wants them as his huntsmen no matter what I say.

Finally, I'd convinced him to let us test out their skills in various disciplines of the profession. He'd balked at first. His mind set on having the huntsmen, and the commander specifically, stay with them it was almost as if he was bewitched. As I think about it now, it feels like he is bewitched. The way he just accepts the commander at his word.

He'd conceded when I pointed out that we may not need all twelve of the huntsmen. That we should look at who were the best among them to keep on at the castle... with the commander. I made sure to include the commander in the group as a mainstay no matter what, he will not give up on that man. I wonder why?

Once he was assured that I had every faith the commander would stay, he left me to devise the testing parameters.

I was grateful for the distraction. It was a change to the endless thoughts that had consumed me the night before.

I watch the huntsmen come out and go through a drill to see who is the best shot. Each of them make their way to the field and one after the other, they hit their targets. I smile when I see the man, Hunter, from the night before, hitting his target in a much better fashion than his commander.

I find myself getting annoyed as Kellen keeps his focus on the commander. The commander isn't even doing that well. All he is doing is borderline flirting with Kellen. While I swing this way, I know that Kellen only has eyes for his one true love, the one he was forced to abandon for the promise he made to his father.

I groan as I see Hunter approaching me. I don't know what he could want, but I have no intention of repeating what happened last night.

He makes eye contact with me as he corners me, smiling. "Why did you kiss me?" He shuffles his feet, and his face starts to turn red. "I mean, I liked it, but why did you do that? Do you like other men?"

I smile, happy he isn't bringing up my shift, I don't let many people see me in my lion form. "How do you know about men liking men, if you didn't even know how to jerk yourself off, last night?"

I can feel my cock start to respond as he fumbles his fingers together, still holding the bow he was practicing with. "I... uh, my sister told me about it... She said it was bad..."

I raise my brow as I find a hole in his story. "How were you able to question your sister, when we aren't allowing you any visitors here?"

The blush that covers his face has me ready to show him more than just how to jerk off... But he saves himself by adding, "It was a long time ago, long before I came here, anyway. She told me after she came back from a bigger city." He wrings his hands around the bow, like he should have done to his cock last night. "I think she thought I was that way, since I hadn't had a girl, I was interested in yet."

This conversation just gets better and better. I raise my eyebrow as I meet his eyes, leaning in close to him, not worried one bit that anyone will see us. "Do you feel that way?"

I watch as his hands freeze on the bow he was holding. "Why would I? I mean, do you feel that way?"

I'm not sure if he's messing with me, or if he is seriously this naive. Either way, I am not going to tell him anything about my feelings. I sure as shit am into him, but if his sister thinks it's bad, then maybe he does too. "Why would I answer that, if you can't tell me how you feel?" I leave the question dangling in the air as he stands there, his mouth open and his eyes darting to the ground.

I walk away, leaving him there, baffled and alone as he thinks about what I've just said. Maybe, hopefully, one day he will come around. Until then, I am keeping my mouth shut. He will have to come to me with his confession, or I won't open up to him about how I feel.

I find myself needing something else to do, so I head to the field and try to come up with another huntsman activity to do. Archery is needed to take down the animals... but can they find the animals they need to shoot?

Having picked which activity they will do tomorrow, I make my way into the castle to let Kellen know my plan. I find myself sighing when I see the commander in the room with him, talking to him like they are old friends, or maybe more.

I groan and clear my throat, trying to get Kellen's attention. When he looks at me, I smile. "I have found the next task the huntsmen will need to prove themselves with." His nod tells me to continue. "Tomorrow we will set up a tracking competition. If that's okay with you, Kellen."

He nods and dismisses me, turning back to this new commander. I have to find out what's gotten into him. I don't know if I will ever figure out who the commander really is, but he isn't who he says he is, and I don't trust him.

CHAPTER THIRTEEN
HUNTER

I look around the field, happy to blow through any test the King has for us. I just hope I trained my sister and her friends good enough to pass as huntsmen. Shaking my head, I listen to Leo as he tells us what the test for the day is.

"Today, each of you will be sent in a different direction in the forest." I hear a round of gasps as the others realize I won't be there to cover for them or help them. "I have set loose twelve different animals into the woods. We will be watching you as you track them, evaluating your technique and grading you." He clears his throat. "The hunt isn't over until each animal I've released is killed and brought back."

With this, he climbs down from the podium, smiling like the cat who got the canary. I find myself gravitating to him as I contemplate yesterday. He ran off from me, ran, after I asked him if he was into men. I didn't answer the question, because I simply don't know. But I do know that I like him.

"I got this; I can track anything."

As I keep thinking about the questions from the day before, I start to think maybe I am ready to answer them today. Taking a deep breath, I head out, following my sister and her friends, who are all following Leo and the King.

Was Leo hurt by my not being able to answer his question? I was just so nervous. I wasn't sure I should answer the questions he was asking, not then. Now that I've had a night to sleep on it, maybe I do know what I want to say.

Leo takes us each to a different starting point, leaving a lower guard with each of the other huntsmen. I'm the last to be positioned, and then a horn is sounded, signaling we are supposed to start our tracking. Immediately, I figure out what it is I am tracking, a boar.

Getting to work, I try to ignore the fact that Leo is always close behind me. Knowing that we have to bring every animal back hunted and field dressed, has me holding my bow at the ready. We are fanned out across the woods, yet Leo is always at my side.

The first question comes as I kneel down, touching the spit-hooved print in the grass. It digs into the dirt just enough to tell me the boar weighs over two-hundred pounds.

"Are you gonna stare at that print all day, or are you gonna shoot the animal?" Leo's voice is a blessing and a distraction.

"I am going to track and kill the boar, just let me do it," I say as I stand up and follow the trail left behind by this not only large, but dangerous animal.

"You're just stalling, you have no idea where or what it is, do you?" Again, his voice is in my ear as he trails right behind me.

I turn around, tired of his shit. "Why are you up my ass? I need you to back off and let me do this." I huff as I turn around again, not sure why this man irritates me so. "Just back off."

He does, for half a second, before he comes back up to me, pulling me to face him. "I don't think you twelve are huntsmen. I think something is wrong with you."

His eyes turn yellow as he holds me in place. Let's face it, there is no way I am moving if he is touching me. Not only is he a strong man, stronger than I can ever hope to be, but he is something... I just can't really tell what it is.

Standing stock still, I meet his eyes. "I am a huntsman, Leo, and I would love for you to let me prove it to you." I look down at our feet, they are so close that they are almost touching. "I can't help what you think, I can only prove what I know of myself. I am now and have always been a huntsmen."

He backs off just a smidge as he huffs. I feel like something is wrong with him, but I can't figure out what it is. His nostrils flare as he turns around. I feel like he has just realized something. I look around the woods, there is no sign that the boar was here recently, we are at least an hour behind it.

Deciding to follow my instincts, I follow Leo instead of the trail. As soon as he hears me behind him, he turns around and grabs my neck, holding it tight, but not in an aggressive way. I see something else in his eyes. A different kind of hunger...

CHAPTER FOURTEEN
LEO

I follow Hunter into the woods, wanting to make sure that there is no cheating going on. I mean, how does one cheat on tracking, I don't know, but there will be someone accompanying each of our huntsmen, just to be sure. I watch as he kneels, evaluating the boar's print in the grass.

I lash out at him and criticize him. Every step of the way this man is making, I correct or make him question his ability as a hunter. That is until I realize he is unflappable at this. I groan as I just get angrier. I almost want to roar. That would scare the boar further into the woods.

Finally, I just let off about my suspicions. Hunter takes them in stride, standing up for himself and focusing on the hunt, proving to me that he is indeed a hunter. I don't know why I am so angry and distracted by this man...

Shit, am I going into rut? There's no way... I turn

towards a cabin as I try to evade this innocent man. He won't know what hit him, if I stay in the same space as him. I feel his eyes on me as he follows me, despite me purposely walking away from the boar's trail.

Turning on him, my hand finds its way to his neck. I won't hurt or kill him, but my hand has a mind of its own, as does my whole body. Staring directly into his eyes, I growl, "I need to go to the cabin, that way." I tilt my head in the direction of it, knowing I don't want to look away. "You need to go back to Kellen and tell him, 'The rut has begun' now, or you won't like what happens next."

I run off to the cabin, feeling Hunter's worry as he bolts in another direction. I need to stop paying attention to him. He will get hurt if he stays with me. Even if he doesn't stay, he is still in danger if the King doesn't get the message.

Getting to the cabin, I lay myself on the bed, stripping my pants off and staring at my raging cock. It looks so hard and angry as I grip it. The relief I feel at the contact of my own hand makes me groan.

I get lost in the feel of my own hand, imagining it's Hunter's ass. That will be the best feeling. I don't know that jerking off is going to stop my rut, but I do know I can't be out there, with that man smelling how he does.

I can still smell him, which only makes me jerk myself harder, gripping my cock and stroking it like it owes me money. The scent of Hunter only gets stronger as I cum, spilling my seed on my stomach.

Having spilled my seed, I take a deep breath in,

smelling him, I can tell he is just outside the cabin door. I told him to leave. Doesn't he get that it's for his safety?

"I told you to go get Kellen! What are you doing back here?" I groan as I feel my cock start to grow with the scent of this man just outside the door.

"Uhh, I ran into one of the other huntsmen... I umm, asked them to pass on the message about rut. I told them I felt like you needed me." He clears his throat. "So, uh, here I am, Leo."

The sound of my name from his lips has me hard as a rock. I just need to jerk off for the foreseeable future, then I can get back to living like a human. "Fuck off, already. I don't need you or your help."

I don't hear him leaving. No, instead I hear him lean against the cabin door. "You were there for me when I was hurt. I don't know what's wrong, Leo, but I want to help you. Can't you just let me?"

Gripping my still rock-hard cock, I get up and make my way to the door. Opening the door, I smirk down at the impatient, and not very obedient Hunter. "Are you willing to help me with this? Because what I really need right now, is someone to fuck." I give a soft roar as his mouth drops open. "If you don't leave, right now, then you are going to be the one I fuck, even if you think it's disgusting." I harden my eyes at him, waiting for him to give me an answer.

The man's mouth closes, and he swallows hard. "I would actually be happy to help you with that. Even though I've never been fucked."

My resolve broken, I grab him by the hand, wrapping

it around my cock. "Are you sure? I will gladly take your virginity, Hunter, but I can't guarantee I will be gentle about it."

The slight nod he gives me, followed by a gentle, too gentle, stroke of my cock is all the permission I need.

CHAPTER FIFTEEN
HUNTER

I wait outside the door, knowing I need to be this man's savior, just like he was mine. His cock is jutting out and I am holding it in my hand as we stand in the doorway of the cabin. His question, the one that has my own cock growing, has me still spinning in my head as he grips my hand tighter, using it to jerk his cock again, but much harder than I just did.

"I'm telling you now, there is no backing out. Once I'm in rut, I need to fuck, and fuck, and fuck again. I will be using you until you can't bear it anymore. And then I will use you some more, Hunter," he says as he pulls me into the house, closing the door and locking it behind me.

"I guess I have no choice now, do I, Leo?" My question is more of a statement, than I realize.

"No, you don't really have a choice, now, Hunter." He strokes his cock with my hand again, this time I can feel a bit more pressure. "I have some oils we can use for lubrication, but that won't help you in the long run.

Tomorrow you will be so sore, you may not be able to walk."

I groan as he strokes himself with my fist, letting me know just how hard he needs it. "I understand, Leo. I will help you with this, no matter how sore I will be in the morning."

He doesn't let my hand leave his cock as I follow him into the cabin, ready and willing to do everything he says. I may not listen to orders I don't want to follow, but I sure feel a need to follow his orders.

His cock seems to get harder as we reach the bedroom. His hand grips my wrist as he directs me to the bed. "I need to get you stretched out, Hunter, you won't be able to take me the first time without help." I swallow hard as he points to the bed. "Get over there and get on your hands and knees." He pauses at the dresser, looking back at me, already on the bed as he says, "If you don't take those clothes off now, I will rip them to shreds."

I smile as I look at my body, still fully clothed. "Oh, sorry."

Getting up, I take my clothes off, quickly so as not to make this man angrier. Who knows what could happen when a shifter is in rut? I don't, but he does, and he sounds serious.

I barely get back in position, before I feel a hand on my naked ass cheek. "Oh!" I shout, startled.

"If that's how you react to a simple touch, just wait til I'm buried deep inside," is all I hear from behind me, before the hand that was on my cheek migrates to the hole that up until this point, was an exit only. I have never put anything in there. "I'm gonna start with my fingers, and some spit, then I'm going to put the oils in." I hear a growl from his throat as his finger finds my hole, pushing in with minimal force. "You're so tight. Relax. I need you to cooperate. I really don't want to hurt you, Hunter."

I take a deep breath in and let it out as he starts to spit on my hole. "Is this better?"

He groans as his spit sits warm on my hole, slowly shoving it in. "A little, but keep breathing, and focus on gripping your cock, like I showed you the other night."

I lean down, letting my shoulders hit the bed, and making my neck very uncomfortable, but I reach for my own cock, squeezing it like he had me squeeze his. "Umm, that feels good."

I almost hear him purring as he slips a second finger into my ass. My cock starts to grow as he does this, and I let myself stroke harder. Squeeze harder. This makes me grunt as he starts spreading his two fingers apart, widening me for himself.

"Good job, Hunter, I think you might be ready." He puts some oil on my ass, it's cold and makes me pucker up again. "Don't worry, I'll warm you up again."

He does just that, slowly slipping his fingers into my hole, this time it goes much easier as he spreads the oils around, relaxing me. When he pulls his fingers away, I groan, missing them in there, knowing that they somehow are meant to be there.

"Don't worry, anxious Hunter, I will fill you," is the last thing I hear before his cock penetrates me.

It hurts and feels good all at once. He's seated himself all the way inside of me, or at least I think he has. His groan of pleasure echoes in the room as he reaches around, taking my cock into his hand.

No more words are said, not for a long time as he does exactly as he promised, filling me, over and over, letting the tip of his cock sit at the entrance of my ass before thrusting in again. This hurts, yet I don't think I ever want him to stop.

I am not a girl, but I sure enjoy the way this man is fucking me. I want him to keep doing this to me for the rest of our lives. Every thrust he gives me makes my cock jump and bead a bit of that sticky stuff that came out before.

The feel of his cock swelling inside of me, has me pushing back against him. He holds me still as he pulses into me, the hot sticky feel of what came out of us before is all over my belly and inside of me. In my ass, to be specific. He lays over top of me, letting our bodies recover. His cock never leaves my ass as he roars, letting more of himself fill me.

He pulls me down, so we are laying on our sides, his cock doesn't leave my ass as he keeps rubbing my now half hard cock. "There, that is just the beginning. At this point your answer is pointless, but are you ready for more?"

I push back into him, as he takes his free hand and wipes some of my sticky fluids up with his pointer finger. "I'm ready, Leo. I can take anything you have to give."

The growl he lets out as he sucks my juices off of his finger has my cock growing again. "I'm glad you said that. We will not be sleeping tonight. Rut takes at least eight hours. I will have moments of clarity, like now, but I will be fucking you relentlessly the rest of the time."

He punctuates his point with a thrust into me again. "I said I will take it, and I will, Leo."

He pulls out of me, and I miss him. I look behind me, thinking I did something wrong, when I look, I see him stroking his cock as he stares into my eyes. "You have a big mouth there, Hunter. Do you want me to fill that next?"

I look at his cock and see that he has wiped it off with the shirt he finally took off his body. "I think I would like that, Leo."

As my mouth is open, saying the last part of his name, he straddles me, not even letting me finish saying his name as he starts to fuck my mouth. "Good. This is gonna hurt just as much as it did in your ass."

I drop my arms and let him in, letting him take what he wants, no, what he needs from my body. I can feel that every inch of me is his now. The way he pounds into my throat should be doing damage, but I know it's not.

Watching as his eyes widen, I swallow around him. "Fuck, that feels good. Do it again, Hunter." I do, but this time I lap my tongue around his shaft and moan as I swallow. "That's it, now again, I'm so close."

Smiling, I do as he says, making my mouth heaven for his cock. This time when I swallow, his stuff spurts out and down my throat. I barely get to taste it, but the feel of it is something I want more of. When he backs out of my throat, I groan, "That was awesome."

His eyes turn into slits as he travels down my body, his cock still hard and at the ready. "I will give you something even more awesome." His mouth works its way down my body as his tongue laps at my sweat. "How would you like your shaft in my mouth?"

I groan as his tongue finds my shaft, licking up it. "I would love that. But how does that help with your rut?"

"Just trust me, Hunter, it does."

With that, his mouth is around me and sucking me off. I am nowhere near as big as him and I fit easily into his mouth as he sucks and laps at me. It reminds me of when he was in his lion form, and he licked up our cum from me.

His eyes meet mine as he sucks hard, pulling more of the sticky goo from me. "Oh, yes, Leo!" I shout as I let go of what's been building up in me since I met him.

His eyes widen as he looks out the window. I see that it is just getting dark, and he surprises me by lifting my legs to his shoulders. "Now that you're all warmed up, Hunter, I am going to rut, and rut, and rut. I won't stop until the sun comes up, if then even."

I swallow hard as his cock lines up with my ass, sliding in like that's where it belongs. The pain is present, but the pleasure overrides it, bringing my cock to attention. Just like his promise, he ruts, and ruts, and ruts into me, until I forget my own damn name.

I never want this night to end...

CHAPTER SIXTEEN
LEO

I sit in the bed, my morning beverage in hand, and my cock out. Yes, I rutted into that hunter all night. I'm certain he will wake up and not even know his name. He looks so peaceful, well fucked and sated.

Finally, when I see the first flicker of realization on his face, I smirk. "You got me through it, Hunter. All night long, you were an accommodating hole to be used, both of your holes, I might add."

His smile widens as he looks over at my cock, getting up on his elbows. "Is this a gift for me, Leo?" I nod as I wait to see what he will do next. "Good, I am sure hungry after all that work last night."

He moans as he slips his lips over me, taking me in as far as he can before swallowing around me. My cock is hard and ready to go, but I don't want to deny him his food, if he wants it in the mouth, I will give him that.

I watch him work, taking all the lessons I gave him last night to the extreme. He licks and he sucks until he milks me of my cum. I smile as he swallows it down. "Are you full, Hunter?"

He blinks slowly twice then nods as he licks his lips. "I am indeed full... but is Hunter my name or am I nameless?"

I laugh at his joke as I pull him into my lap, setting the cup I'm holding on the stand next to the bed. "You're my Hunter. I don't care what happens from here out, Hunter, you are mine." I kiss his lips, pulling him as close to me as we can possibly get. "You're just the perfect fit for me."

He moans as my still hard cock rubs against his back. "Ready again?"

I smirk as I rub his chest. "I am always ready for you, Hunter. The real question, is... Are you ready to be fucked?"

His nod has me flipping him, onto his back as he lets his legs relax, giving into me and opening up for me. I slide my hand down his body as I take in every inch of this well fucked man. His cock stands at attention, just as much as mine does.

Kneeling between his legs I take his cock into my mouth, sucking on him and letting him know that he is allowed pleasure too. His moan sets my cock to bobbing as he thrusts into my throat. I hum and lap at his cock until I think he can't take it anymore, then I make a popping noise as I back off his cock.

"You are really tasty, Hunter." I grip his calves as I angle him just right, lining my cock up with his spread and exposed ass. No lube he's still dripping with my cum from last night. It's messy as hell. "But I love to fuck you, hard." I meet his eyes as I hold his legs still. "You will let me, won't you, Hunter?"

He moans and wiggles his ass as I pull back, then slam deep into him, watching as he spreads wider, accepting my girth and my length. The tightness of his asshole around me has me grunting, and barely able to hold back. I think I am in love.

The rut, it must have been caused by him, his nearness. The way he smells loaded with my cum, is even better than I could imagine. I give him my all, watching pleasure span his face as I hit his most sensitive spot, over and over. When he cums on his own stomach, I groan, letting my seed spill uselessly into his ass.

If this is what life is, I never want to stop living it. I am guard to a king, though, so I need to go back to my job at some point. I pull out of Hunter, letting my cum drip from his pulsing asshole. I watch as the bed gets covered in it.

I pull away from the bed, shifting into my lion form. Hunter startles, but only momentarily as he watches me closely. I growl low in my chest as I lick up both his cum and my own. This is the most effective way to clean up our messes. His cock jumps under the roughness of my tongue, and the nearness of my sharp canines to his most valued body part.

Unable to resist, I nip at his tip, making sure not to hurt him, I would like to use that again later. The fear in his eyes is quickly replaced with relaxation as he gives in to the roughness of my tongue, letting me lick him completely clean.

Still in my lion form, I sit on the bed and lick myself

clean, growling as Hunter reaches out and pets my mane. His hand doesn't leave me as he kneels next to me. "Can you understand me?" I nod, not able to talk, but able to understand. "I think I love you."

As he says it, he wraps his arms around my neck, not fearing me in the least as he holds me close. I can't help that my cock grows as he holds me close, his body still fully naked.

When he finally lets go, I have already shifted back to my human form. "Now look what you've gone and done. My cock is all hard again."

He doesn't hesitate, just leans over me, taking my cock in his mouth, as he licks and sucks, making me cum deep in his throat. He licks his lips as he smiles. "There, all better. Now what's on the agenda today? Did I fail your hunting thing? I mean I can get back out and track that boar down."

I focus on him as I get up and start to get dressed again. "You didn't fail, I pulled you away from the competition. Let's see how your crew did."

His face shifts and I suspect he wants to say something, but we don't have a lot of time. The sun is out, and I have been away from my king for far too long. "Okay, I guess," he says as he too gets dressed.

Once we are dressed, we head out into the woods, making our way to the castle. I, of course, know exactly where we are going, but I hold his hand, letting him lead the way back. This man is great at directions, and he needs to be on our team. He needs to be one of our huntsmen.

Every once in a while, on the way back to the castle, I

pull him in for a kiss, holding him at the back of the neck. I don't want him to be afraid to be with me. I am not afraid of who I am. I love men, and I always have. As we reach the castle, Hunter pulls away from me, smiling. "As much as I love making out with you in public, I need to find my sis... uh, the other huntsmen."

Did I hear what I think I did? Probably not. "Fine, go see what they are doing. I will catch up with you later." I pull him in for one last kiss. As I watch him make his way to the huntsmen quarters, my cock grows again. I think I may be in a semi-perpetual rut with him around.

I need to get out to find the king anyway. I have no idea what he could have gotten into. I make my way through the castle, landing in the cafeteria. My mouth drops as I take in what I am seeing.

The king, my king, Kellen, is sitting in his spot at the table, smiling and kissing one of the huntsmen. It's that crafty commander of theirs. I know that Kellen is not one who favors men, like I do. Why is he kissing this man? What happened to the love he was pining over?

"What the fuck is going on, Kellen?" Kellen pulls away from the huntsmen's commander, wiping some spit from his lips.

"I... well, it's a long story."

I put my hands on my hips, not sure what could have led to this. "I have a long time..."

"You see, you were right, there was something off about these huntsmen. They are not men at all. This is CiCi."

I tilt my head as I look and see a man in front of me. "That is a man; last I checked, CiCi was a woman."

He smiles as he tosses something to me. "Do you remember this?" I nod, recognizing the ring that he gave to CiCi. "I went to check on this huntsman, since he was hurt." His eyes meet the huntsman's as he continues, "I found the ring in his pocket. When she saw that I found the ring, she came clean."

I tilt my head, still confused, as I try to figure out what this all means. "Came clean?"

"Yeah, she told me all about how she heard that I was getting married to someone else. She was so desperate to find me, that she took a potion."

"A potion?" I can't believe what I'm hearing, but the more I smell this man, the more I realize that he is just masking, he really is a woman.

"Yeah, a potion that made her and her sister, and their friends men. He's really a she. They have something with them to turn them back into women." He looks at her smiling. "Right?" When she nods, he continues, "I just know that my promise to her is more important than the one I made to my dad. I am going to marry CiCi like I had originally planned to." His eyes turn to me as he asks, "Can you accept that, Leo? Can you support me in my true love?"

CHAPTER SEVENTEEN
HUNTER

I find myself in the huntsmen chambers, they are abuzz with conversation, and the girls all sound upbeat. I look around at all of them, minus my sister, of course. She has been spending every waking moment with the King. I groan as I think about Leo, my cock is responding even without me wanting it to.

Laticia comes up to me patting me on the shoulder. "We did it."

I look over at her. "What's all the noise about? What did we do?"

Laticia smiles as she twirls like a woman showing off a dress. "CiCi, she told the King everything. King Kellen knows we are women."

I feel a bolt of fear shoot through my body. "He knows?" If he knows then it's only a matter of time before Leo realizes it too.

"Yes, he knows everything. CiCi is with him right now, sitting in the cafeteria. I can't believe that he knows, even though she has the ring to prove it is her, I still never thought we would pull this off." Laticia looks at the other girls. "We should celebrate. Plan a big ole Castle ball."

"How did he find out?" I ask, still dumbfounded.

"King Kellen came to check on her and saw the ring. That was all the proof he needed, that and the amazing connection they have to one another."

Her words fall to deaf ears as I think about the consequences this may have on me and Leo. I really do love the man. But would he love me as a woman? King Kellen seems to love CiCi even though she is a man right now.

I'm snapped out of the painful thought when I feel a hand on my shoulder. "You know what that means, Diana."

I cringe at the name. It's just not who I see myself as anymore. Let's face it, I never saw myself as Diana. I have always been Hunter. I have always been a man. What happens if I don't chew the one prescribed leaf?

Holding the leaf I am supposed to take, I look at all the others, turning into women as they each take their own, chewing them and swallowing. I don't want to be a woman. I want to be Leo's man. I want to be Hunter. I want to stay Hunter.

I look at the leaf, putting it on the dresser, instead of taking it. I know that Leo won't want me as a woman, so I run. Leaving the leaf behind, I run, as far and fast as I can. Once he knows that I am not, nor have I ever truly been a man, I will be off his list.

He won't want a woman. I saw how much he hungered for my cock, for my cum. I saw everything he offered me as a man. His rut was for me. He knows it as much as I do. I find an opening in the woods and head down that path.

At least if I am not anywhere near him, I can pretend that the man still wants me, still loves me. Running is the only thing on my mind as I bolt through the woods. I forget all about the wild animals that have been left to get hunted in these woods and just run. I do still, as always, have my bow. It never leaves me.

Yeah, I will just leave. I don't want to... No, I can't handle his rejection, when he sees I no longer have a penis. I won't. I refuse to let him see that.

CHAPTER EIGHTEEN
LEO

I nod absent mindedly. "Yeah, I can support that." Something hits me smack in the chest. "Wait, are all your huntsmen, women?"

CiCi smiles as she nods. "Yeah, Hunter is my sister, Diana." She looks lost in thought. "Although, he was asking some weird questions the other night. Things like, 'do you think you can be born in the wrong body?' and 'is it okay to love someone the same gender as you feel?'" Her shrug has me anxious. "It was weird. Why do you ask?"

I wave my hand at her, uh, him? And just walk away. I don't think I can handle this conversation anymore. I feel like they are just going to bring me down.

The rut I had last night was with a man. I know it. I wonder if he is going to chew on the leaf to change back? Is he really a she? Deep down inside?

As I'm pacing, I hear CiCi speak up, "You know, Diana has always seemed like a man. It was so much easier for her to pass as a man than it was for us. Do you think…"

I cut her words off, growing angry at her use of Hunter's old name. "It's Hunter. He is named Hunter."

The look I get makes me even more angry as I pace in the room. "Well, Diana is going to have to turn back to a woman, it's the leaf we have to chew," says CiCi.

"No, CiCi. You are a woman; you have a woman's name. Hunter is not. He smells like a man. He is a man. He may have even known it his whole life. I'm telling you now, Hunter is no woman. Hunter is a man. The man for me. The only man for me."

With that I race off, running through the halls in search of the man I love. I sniff the air as I run through the castle. Finding the huntsmen chambers, I rush in, failing to knock. I smell the air. Hunter was here, I don't know how long ago, but he was.

His scent makes my cock grow, which is unusual with all these women around. They rarely turn me on. Some of these huntsmen are still men, some are women. The one who sees me laughs as she says, "I'm so happy to be free of that manly body." I shrug her off as she starts to flirt with me. "Maybe now you will accept me. I thought you were hot from the moment we met."

Her eyes widen as I shove her off me and sniff the air. Hunter's scent is still out there. Still lingering. I need to find him. Seeing a leaf on the dresser, I ask, "Is this it, what you take to turn back?" When the flirty woman nods, I grab it and bolt. The chatter they make as I leave tells me more than one of them were interested in me.

None of them interest me, never have. The only real man in the group was... no is Hunter. I need to find him.

Knowing that he took off, probably because he didn't

want to become a woman, become Diana, again, I rush after his scent. He may not realize it, but my lion will track him down no matter how far he gets.

Based on the time I spent interrogating CiCi and Kellen, and the scent left here, I know he's been gone at least an hour. I groan as I hit the grass, shifting into my lion form. I don't care who sees me. I am going to find my man.

I am happy I grabbed the leaf meant to help them transform, when I left the women behind. All of them had taken theirs. I know Hunter didn't. The one with his scent on it was the only one left behind.

Running through the woods in my lion form, has me even more determined to find him. The air of him rushes through me as I run in the woods, tracking him and his scent. Stopping at a tree, I sniff. He leaned against this one.

I rub my chin and cheek against it, marking this man as mine. This tree, his scent. All of it is mine. I am a very possessive lion, as Hunter will learn.

He is now becoming the hunted. I will not give up. I don't care if I have to chase him for months. I will find him. King Kellen will just have to deal without me.

CHAPTER NINETEEN
HUNTER

I find myself still running. The woods rip by me and my ankle still hurts off and on. I run through the pain, that's what us men do. Having left the leaf, I was meant to take behind, I have no idea what's going to happen to me. Will the potion wear off?

I have no idea what will happen, but I do know that as long as I have my manly body, I will keep moving. I will keep the name Hunter. I love it. I just wish I could keep Leo.

Pushing the sad thought from my mind, I stop and lean against a tree. I can feel the sweat dripping off my body as I take a break. Hearing something off in the woods, I stand up straight, alert.

That was an animal, for sure. I wonder how many of the game that Leo released we caught? I don't know how well my few arrows will hold up against a herd of wild boar, assuming that's what he released.

Cautiously, I move away from the tree, this time fear

floods my veins as I hear a snort. I need to get out of these woods, before I wind up hog's stew.

Logically, I know that they will smell the fear on me. I don't care. I need to run. Run I do, right into the depths of the woods. The further I go, the more I think this is a bad idea. We traveled a great distance to get to the castle, I know my way around the woods. But I have none of my equipment. Not even a compass.

I sigh as I listen to the sounds around me. More silence greets me. Then I hear it, a grunt, low in the throat of an animal. I turn around to see a hog, its beady eyes are staring me down and he is too close for me to shoot with my arrows.

I can move faster than him, I can climb, but in this moment, I find that I can't really do any of that. Frozen in place, I slowly draw my arrow from my quiver, risking it and quickly drawing my bow. The hog starts at me again, but before it can reach me, my arrow pierces its heart.

The fear running through my veins only intensifies as I hear more hogs running up behind me. I'm trapped and I can't get out of this one. No amount of arrows will get them all. I am a great hunter, but I am not that great.

I resigned myself to my fate, ready to give up and call it. That is, until I hear a loud roar. Leo. It has to be him.

My senses coming back to me, I shoot the two closest to me, then make my way up the nearest tree. From up here, I can see the man, no, lion of my dreams, running in my direction. His nose is in the air and his roar comes again, scattering the gathered hogs.

All but one brave one who scrapes the ground and faces Leo. I can almost feel the chuckle he would give as he sees the hog. I thought maybe I could start a new life, one where I never was a woman, one where I didn't have to lie to everyone around me.

But looking at the way Leo handles this hog, I realize I have no other choice. I need to face this man, I need to be the man he thinks I am. Telling him the truth is my only option. Still, I hop down from the tree and run. I may still be able to get away, to become someone else. It could work. No one would have to know.

Then, when the illusion wears off, I can go back to my dad and be the spinster I was always destined to be. "Yeah, that could wo..."

CHAPTER TWENTY
LEO

I can smell the fear building in Hunter's scent. He is alone in the woods, and I know that those women did not catch any of the hogs. Each one of them alone are a formidable force, but them as a herd, he doesn't stand a chance.

I keep running at my top speed, chasing this man, hoping I get to him before I start to smell his blood. I roar, hoping to scare off any of the remaining hogs. When I hear the squeals, all coming from the same direction, I look up into the tree, seeing a still very male Hunter trapped in a tree. Just where I want him.

The hog at the base of the tree charges me, giving it his all as the man is left to his resources in the tree. I ignore him, thinking he will stay right there. This hog needs a lesson in challenging a lion.

It takes me no time at all to take the hog down. I eat his heart and then his liver, before abandoning him for later. I can always use a fresh kill. But I have bigger priorities on my agenda.

Looking up at the tree, I see that Hunter is no longer where I left him. That silly man. Why must he run from me?

I sniff the air and listen for the crunching of feet on leaves. Finding him is no chore when his scent is part of me now. I race to him, listening as I approach him. He is saying something, "Yeah, that could wo..."

I cut him off, my prey drive taking over. He falls to the ground, and I lick his face, enjoying the taste of his fear. He looks up at me, holding his hands out. "Leo, Is that you?"

He's kinda dumb if he thinks asking a real big cat if its who he thinks it is, would stop them. Rubbing my face against him, I start to do my best to purr in his ear.

I can feel the tension leaving his body as he accepts my rubbing. My lion cock is growing, and I know there is so much more to be discussed. I have to stop licking and rubbing on him, before I lose control again.

Still standing over him, I shift, leaving my hands on his shoulders, where my front paws were. "Yes, you idiot. I am Leo. The questions are now mine to ask." I look at him, waiting for him to argue, but his eyes drop down to my cock. I smile knowing it is full for him and him alone. "Don't worry about that. We need to talk, Hunter."

His voice is ragged as he says, "What is there to talk about? You already know everything. If the King knows, then so do you. That's how close you are with him."

I growl at him, unable to resist kissing him again. "I don't know everything. I know what your sister, the commander, said. I know what Kellen said. What I don't know is how you feel."

Before he can answer I steal another kiss, looking into his eyes as he starts, "I feel like a man. I want to be a man. I feel like no man will want me. As a woman I had no suiters."

I cut him off right there, with another forceful kiss. "I know that what I feel for you, Hunter, is real. I know that you are the man I have wanted for a long time."

"Yeah, but now you know that I wasn't a man before this. No matter how much I want to be a man, I can't just be one forever. At some point this potion will wear off and I will become a woman again. I will become Diana," the name is said with such disdain that I can't resist kissing him again. He shakes his head, continuing, "Even if you did want me as a woman, you wouldn't want me. Because no man wants a wife that would rather hunt than knit and sew his clothes."

I can see the pain in his eyes as I keep him pinned in place, my cock jutting out for him. "I can see why you would think that."

He ignores my comment, continuing, "I know you don't want a wife who can beat you in archery, Leo. Why can't you just let me go be miserable?"

I look at him and smile. "Hunter, I want you, no matter what form you take." I pull the leaf that was left behind out from under my tongue. Yes, it's been there the whole time. "Take this, then I can see what form my love, my Hunter, will take. I love you, even if you turned into a hog, I would still love you..."

I glance back at the gutted hog, my guts rumbling for more food. "I guess I can take that as a compliment." He grabs the leaf with the hands I just freed, as I walk a short distance from him, ready to see what this leaf is supposed to do.

I watch as he chews the leaf, seeming to not like the flavor of it. I'm sure my saliva has gotten on it too. As he swallows down the last of the leaf, I say, "For what it's worth, you never smelled like a woman to me. You always have smelled like Hunter."

I watch as the leaf does nothing. For all of ten minutes, I stare at the clothed form of my love, my Hunter. My cock grows with anticipation as I wait to see if he will change, knowing deep down that he won't.

CHAPTER TWENTY-ONE
HUNTER

I take the leaf that I left behind on purpose, chewing on it, the flavor of it mixes with Leo's lion spit, and maybe some blood. This man so won't take no for an answer. If he says he'll love me as a woman, then I guess it's worth the chance. I think I feel something. At the very least it feels like enough time has passed for me to have changed already.

Not hearing a word from Leo, I turn myself away from him, hiding in shame. I knew he wouldn't like me as a woman. Sensing what's coming, I start to walk away.

The next second I feel Leo's hand on my shoulder. "You're still a man, Hunter. I knew it. I knew that you really are a man." He breathes me in, his nose lining up with my neck. At that moment, I remember that he is completely naked behind me. "You smell so good, Hunter."

I feel his cock hard against my back right before he turns me to face him. "What are you doing, Leo?"

He doesn't say a word, just pulls me into a kiss, making me feel all the feelings I thought I would lose when I became a woman again. When the illusion gets lifted. But he said I was still a man. His hand guides mine down to his bare cock. I groan as I feel the hardness of his shaft in my hands.

With my hand firmly in place on his cock, Leo grips my very hard cock, groaning as he feels how heavy it is. The way I can feel his hand gripping me, I know that I do still have the right equipment to be who I have always wanted to be.

"Is that my?"

"Your cock? Yes, Hunter, that is your cock, and I am happy to prove to you that it works just fine."

I push him away sighing as I look down, seeing his cock and mine, both very hard with desire for each other. "You must have given me the wrong leaf."

He grabs my face, making me look into his eyes. "No, I made sure it was the same one your sister's friends took. This is the real you, Hunter." He kisses my lips as he thrusts his hips forward, letting me feel his hardness against my own. "Now, just lay back and enjoy this with me."

I push him away, not sure what else to do. "No, maybe it just takes longer to take effect. I know for sure I was a woman. The illusion is that I am a man, Leo. I know I'm not a man, I can't be. I was born a girl."

He stops my rant, pulling me against himself as he kisses me. I give in, letting myself have this moment as I get kissed silly. As he pulls back, he grips my cock. "You are a man, Hunter. Let me prove it to you." He shrugs.

"Besides, all the others are back to women, or at least all of them that I noticed. If it took longer, why would they have already been out of the illusion?"

I look at him letting his words sink in. My body still is reacting to him as he gets on his knees, letting my pants loose. "What are you doing?"

He looks me in the eyes. "I'm taking care of my man. That's what you are, Hunter, my man."

By the time he is down on his knees, I can feel my cock hanging out, heavy with an erection. In seconds his mouth is over it, proving to me more and more that my cock is very real.

I groan with pleasure as he sucks on me harder, his smile telling me just how much he is enjoying himself. "But it can't be true."

Leo's mouth leaves my cock just long enough for him to ask, "Why don't you think it is true?"

I moan at the loss of his mouth on my cock, before groaning in pleasure again. "I have always wished to be a man. I feel like if I had always wished to be a man..." I drift off as he grips my testicles, his pointer finger making its way to my asshole. "What I'm trying to say is that I was born a woman, so I will always be one, right?"

Leo grips my ass cheeks spreading them apart as he uses his own strength to pull me towards him. After gagging on my cock, he smiles up at me. "Would a woman be able to gag me with her cock?"

I look down as he slips me into his mouth again, enjoying the way my cock fits in his throat, I grab the back of his head, thrusting, as I hold him still. "No, she wouldn't." I tilt my head back as I lose myself in the distraction of Leo's hungry mouth. "Ugh, I…"

Leo smacks my ass, drawing me away from what I was saying. I look down to see his eyes focused on mine. I don't need to hear him say it, to know that he wants me to just stop talking and take the mouth he is offering to me.

I do just that, thrusting hard and fast as I hold his head in place. I'm not a woman. I never was. I may have been born with a woman's parts, but that witch's potion brought out my true self, not the illusion.

As more proof of this, I feel my cock start to pulse as Leo swallows around it. My body is shuddering with the intensity of the orgasm Leo just gave me. I fall to my knees, looking Leo in the eyes as he holds either side of my face.

"I'm a man."

Leo smiles at my declaration. "Yes, Hunter, you are. You always smelled of a man since to moment I met you. Your sister didn't. But you did." He kisses me, letting my flavor linger on our lips. "Now you get it, Hunter."

He smiles as he kisses me again, before pushing me down on the ground. "What did I do?"

Leo laughs behind me as he slaps my ass. "You didn't do anything, besides give me the taste of you again. Now though, I am going to fuck my man. I will make sure he never doubts his manly traits again."

With my ass in the air and my head getting pushed into the grass, I moan. "Okay."

I barely get the word out before he kneels behind me, slipping his cock into my ass. No warmup is needed, since I am still thoroughly stretched from his rut the night before.

Yes, I am a man. Yes, I am getting fucked by a man, who is sometimes a lion. Both of these things can be true. They are both true.

This time as he fucks me, I feel the love that was missing in the rut. There was love, but it wasn't like this. This time I can feel his love for me, in the slow way he takes me.

Here we are, two men rutting in the woods. My life is complete. But what will my sister think?

After all this activity, and feeling drained, I look into Leo's eyes. "Should we get back to the castle?"

He nods. "Yes, we should."

He stands up and shifts, licking us clean, before I pick up my clothes and get dressed. I smile as he crouches down in his lion form, letting me climb on his back to ride him to the castle. The whole way there, I wonder what will happen when I see my sister again.

It seems she was waiting for me. Her eyes widen only slightly when she sees me coming in on the back of a lion. "Leo, where the hell was my sister, and why is she still a he?"

Leo shakes his hairy body, letting me off his back as I march up to CiCi. "I'm still a man, because I really am a man."

She looks at Leo, still in his lion form. "Okay, give her the leaf, the jig is up, Leo."

I look into her eyes, knowing I chewed and swallowed the leaf the witch told us to. "Really, CiCi. I've taken it and I am really a man." I smile as I add, "You remember how I said I always felt like a man, that's because, at heart, I really am." I take a breath before continuing, "The potion didn't change me back, that means I really am a man." I turn her to face me. "Are you willing to accept me as a man who likes other men?"

My sister smiles as she looks at Leo, now a human again, fully dressed. "And you picked this man? The one who turns into a lion?" I nod and she sighs. "Yes, brother, Hunter, I will accept you as you are. Man, body and all."

Leo asks, "What exactly did the witch say when you got the potion and leaves?"

I repeat word for word what she said to us, and Leo's face lights up. "That's the reason I didn't smell the same changes in Hunter as I did the rest of you. His potion was a truth potion. It brought his true self out. The other potions for the rest of you were the illusions."

CiCi seems to accept this answer as she shouts, "Let's have a celebratory dinner."

Kellen is right behind her, making his presence known as he says, "I'm glad you found love too Leo."

EPILOGUE

LEO

The last two weeks have flown by. Kellen wanted a rushed wedding. He didn't want to wait any longer to be with his bride, the one he chose, not the one he told his dad he would marry.

Of course, he's chosen me as his best man. I smile as I see all of the people of our kingdom gathered for this event. The wedding of the King is something they aren't allowed to miss.

I look at all the chaos going on, knowing that Kellen is ready to marry his love. It gets me thinking about marrying the love of my life. Just because he's a man, doesn't mean I shouldn't be allowed to marry him too.

I feel a pinch in my heart at the thought that I won't

be able to marry Hunter one day. The feeling spoiled, I head towards Kellen. "Are you ready for this? I know you have been waiting ages to marry her. CiCi really is perfect for you."

Kellen's eyes light up as he hears me reference her by name. "Yes, she is the best thing that has ever happened to me. I will stand here all day and wait for her to be ready." He leans towards me as he adds, "Why don't you go tell your boy toy not to rush her."

I smile at the fact that the King, my King, Kellen, is fully aware of my love for not only men in general, but for this one man in particular. If anyone can see that the rules around here need changing, its him. "Sure thing, Kellen. Oh, and he's not just a toy, I love that man."

He shrugs as the bliss makes its way back to his face. "I know. I was just messing with ya."

I head off in the direction of the bride's chambers, knowing that Hunter will be in there with CiCi, helping her get ready.

HUNTER

I smile as I watch my sister getting ready for her wedding. We really made it all happen. Not only did she find the love of her life, but I found mine too.

He is a strong lion of a man, one who takes charge of

me most nights. There hasn't been a night in the past two weeks that I haven't slept in his bed.

"I don't see how you can resist sleeping with Kellen. I can't get enough of Leo."

CiCi's eyes find mine in the mirror as she shrugs. "Why do you think we pushed the date up. We can't wait any longer."

Her eyes are filled with hope and expectation. "Okay, I guess that's fair."

She swats my hand as I slow down on fixing up her hair. I've never really been good at this stuff. "Why don't you do this faster? I want to get out there and marry my man, Hunter."

I shake my head as I rush it, knowing that it will never be perfect with me doing her hair anyway. When I finish the braid, I was working on, I dust my hands off. "Well, is that how you wanted it?"

She pats her hair, looking only for a moment longer in the mirror. Then there is a sharp rapping at the door. "Who is it?" coos my sister.

"It's Leo, the best man, Kellen says not to rush you but..."

He doesn't get to finish his sentence as CiCi finds her way to the door, opening it and running towards the area she will marry Kellen at. "I wanna be rushed, Leo."

With that, she grabs our dad's hand. Well, he still hasn't said much about my change. CiCi told him that this is who I am, but he doesn't seem to notice either way. I shiver as Leo touches me.

"So, your sister seems to be in a rush. We are

supposed to be up there before she is, ya know, so Kellen gets a heads up that she's coming."

I shrug as I take his hand. "I'm fine with that. Kellen knows what he's getting into." Kissing him, I bring him closer to me, letting our cocks touch through the fabric that covers them. "Don't you wish we could get married too?"

His face lights up as he says, "Yeah, I really do. Maybe since we have the King's ear, we will be able to set a new precedent."

I can feel the anxiety rushing through me as my dad comes back, putting a hand out for me. "Well, what are you waiting for?"

I tilt my head as I try to figure out what he means. "What's going on?"

A look at a shrugging Leo, tells me that he has no idea what's going on either. I loop my hand through my dad's arm and let him lead me. Kellen signals to Leo, and he runs up to him, to be sure everything is okay.

The way his eyes widen when Kellen whispers in his ear, tells me something is up. I groan as I look at my dad. "What is it? Why are you walking me down the aisle, dad?"

He smiles. "You may be my son now, but that man, Leo, he is waiting for you."

Still confused, I'm passed over to Leo, as the crowd cheers. We stand there as Kellen clears his throat, announcing to the kingdom, something I thought I would never hear, "Today I will marry my love, this is very true. But we are also here to witness history as I am sanctioning the first man to man wedding here, with my right-hand man and his boyfriend."

Leo seems just as shocked as I feel. I barely hear a word as we say our vows and let the world know that we are committing ourselves to each other.

Just a few short months, that's all it took to get our lives turned upside down. I went from an out of place woman, feeling like a man; to a man, marrying another man. I couldn't be any happier if I tried.

ABOUT AMELIA HAYDEN

Amelia Hayden is a sassy, crazy, romance fanatic that loves love in all its forms.

When she's not writing about romance, she's binge watching Schitt's Creek for the hundredth time. Dan Levy is her idol, spirit animal, possible obsession, because she adores anyone who can pull off sarcastically witty lines like others may say "Hi."

If you love that too, along with steamy, sexy, kinky fun times mixed in with a dash (aka massive handfuls) of romance then you'll fall in love with Amelia Hayden.

Find my socials here (www.romanceequality publishing.com).

ALSO BY AMELIA HAYDEN

Wynn (Single Dads of Gaynor Beach Series)

Nate (Single Dads of Gaynor Beach Series)

Saved by the Everyday Hero (A limited edition romance collection)

The Baker and his Curvy Customer (Curves on Demand)

Sin Bin: A MM Sports Romance Novel (Playing for Keeps)

Kwan: A Contemporary K-Pop Rockstar Romance (2 Hot 2 Handle Shared World)

Coming Soon

Blitz Defense: A MM Sports Romance Novel (Playing for Keeps)

ONCE UPON A TIME
THE SERIES

Men of might and magic find true love in this multi-author novella and novel-length M/M+ fairytale reimagining series featuring fairies, werewolves, fae princes, vampires, orcs, mermen, and more, available in Kindle Unlimited and to purchase at amazon.com/dp/B0CC2ZQJX9.

RELEASE DATES:

Imprisoned by the Wizard by Zelda Knight (March 31, 2024)

Graced by the Cat by Geneva Holt (April 8, 2024)

Chased by the Fairy by Opal Reyne (April 22, 2024)

Hunted by the Lion by Amelia Hayden (June 15, 2024)

Stalked by the Giant by Lexi Ostrow (June 22, 2024)

Owned by the Outlaw by Kinkaid Knight & Zelda Knight (June 29, 2024)

Magicked by the Mirror by Juniper Kerry (July 8, 2024)

Worshipped by the Wolves by Kelly Lord (July 18, 2024)

Entranced by the Immortal by R.K. Pierce (July 25, 2024)
Cursed by the Crown by R.K. Pierce (August 2, 2024)